The First Tree in the Greenwood

Book Thirteen of the *Coming Back to Cornwall* series

Katharine E. Smith

HEDDON PUBLISHING

www.heddonpublishing.com
www.facebook.com/heddonpublishing
@PublishHeddon

Katharine E. Smith is the author of twenty-three novels. *The First Tree in the Greenwood* is the thirteenth Coming Back to Cornwall book.

The Connections series is also set in Cornwall, with each story focusing on a different character but each tale linked inextricably to the others. Katharine's most recent series is What Comes Next and is set – for a change – in Shropshire, where she lives with her husband, their two children, and two excitable dogs.

A Philosophy graduate, Katharine initially worked in the IT and charity sectors. She turned to freelance editing in 2009, which led to her setting up Heddon Publishing, working with independent authors across the globe.

You can find details of her books on her website:
www.katharineesmith.com

Information about her work with other authors can be found here:
www.heddonpublishing.com
and here:
www.heddonbooks.com

For Gill
with love, thanks and admiration
xxx

The First Tree in the Greenwood

How is it possible that it's Christmas time again? I'm still mourning the passing of summer but I think that says more about me than how fast time flies. I have to work hard not to be a misery about winter moving in – I don't want to infect Ben or Holly with my seasonal Scrooge-ness. And I do love it as far as Christmas, even as an adult with sleep deprivation which will only get worse over the next week or so – crescendoing to the Big Day itself when at last the ever-inflating balloon of craziness will reach its peak and inevitably burst. Then comes Boxing Day when the whole country will sigh with collective relief, that it's over for another year, that there is no more having to remember last-minute presents or somehow make a Christmas dinner for twelve when the oven's packed in. The worrying over the family arguments will be over and guests, whether welcome or tolerated, will begin to return to their own homes, restoring normal order to households.

And yes, I know I said I love Christmas and yet that all sounds very miserable. But there's no denying it can be a time fraught with stress and overtiredness and the pressure of making everything perfect. Balancing expectations against reality. But I do love Christmas, really, and I loved it even more as a child. There is something about the nights closing in early, cocooning the world until well into the morning; the warm, twinkling lights we string along the streets and around our trees and houses, to take away the sting of the darkness, making it cosy as opposed to sinister or bleak. I do love getting to bed early without feeling guilty; a book and a duvet and Sam's warm body next to me.

The magical tales, both old and new, of Father

Christmas/Saint Nick/Santa, and woodland creatures, and fairytale heroes and villains, good warding off bad. And the feeling that we have crossed the threshold of winter, too, the solstice marking the turn back towards the light. Even though in reality it is a long time before we will notice any difference.

My parents went to great lengths to ensure that the magic settled over our family home when I was a child, and Sam – though he says his Christmases were not quite the same as mine – is as determined to do the same for our children as I am.

But there is never any guarantee. Given that it's meant to be a time of peace and good will, we've had some quite dramatic Christmases, although not quite in the same catastrophic vein of *Eastenders* or *Coronation Street*. Even so, there was the year that Sam and I nearly split up, when we'd barely even got back together. And Holly's miraculous birth, stranded by snow at Amethi, with the small matter of a possible Christmas ghost mixed in. And of course last year, when the drama was really Natalie's, not ours. We were just bystanders who managed to involve ourselves, but I know Natalie is grateful that we did. And now, as a result of it, we have a lovely family of friends living just doors away – and a new dog. Though I still miss Meg, so much.

"You shouldn't have tried to replace Meg so quickly," Karen unhelpfully told me when Poppy, still settling in, had weed on the kitchen floor.

"We're not replacing her," Sam and I had responded in unison – he bristling even more than me; Karen, being his mum, can really press his buttons and even more when he knows she's upsetting me.

Poppy was Sam's idea anyway – decided upon without consulting me, but with the very best intentions. He knew, or at least hoped, she would be a comfort for me, and a distraction, when Julie was heading back to Canada. And she gives me a reason to get out every day – often with Natalie, who has Poppy's son Keith. Yes, Keith. And in comparison to the whirlwind of mayhem that puppy is, the odd wee on the kitchen floor from Poppy is nothing.

Anyway, she is much more settled now, and I'm so glad to have her. Not, as Karen suggested, as a replacement for Meg – there could be no such thing – but as an addition to our family. And Ben and Holly love her too, of course. When they went back to school, we had the joy of walking Poppy along to the gates, where she got a lot of attention and now clearly craves it, pulling towards most people we see in the expectation they will want to make a fuss of her.

Back in September, I would drop the children off and then take Poppy down to the dog-friendly beach, with the dog ban still in place on the others, or wander along the harbourside which was already quieter than a few weeks before, the tide of summer holiday-makers having turned. It was still warm and sunny back then, I can't help thinking wistfully. When the school day was finished we could pretend it was still the summer holidays, dumping school bags in the hallway and picking up a bag I'd prepared earlier, *Blue Peter*-style, heading back down to the little beach and all of us enjoying a paddle – or a swim in Ben's case, after a bit of negotiation with me.

Having Holly to watch, and still not 100% sure of what

Poppy is like with other dogs and/or people, I'd have been struggling to help him if he got into any trouble. But he's a strong swimmer, and we have taught him well, so he understands the risks and doesn't push things or stray too far from the shoreline. He just loves swimming, and I completely understand that. In fact, I was a little bit envious; I'd have loved to have joined him. Instead, I would watch from the shore, part of me planning for what I would do if he did need my help; part of me just enjoying seeing the smile on his face.

As the months have gone on, those after-school beach visits are a thing of the past but, as with every year, holiday season has retreated even further and the late winter months are some of the least popular for visitors. It's been a joy to be allowed back on all the beaches with the dogs again, enjoying the kind of space you could only dream of in July and August, as well as some unexpectedly warm weather here and there.

I do miss those afternoons with the children playing on the sand until it's time to go home for tea, but it's just too dark and cold and windy and/or rainy at that time of the afternoon these days. Besides, most of Ben's afternoons have been tied up practising for the great primary school play extravaganza that the older kids do instead of a nativity. This year it was a version of *The Muppets Christmas Carol* and Ben had the part of one of the critics. Apparently he is Waldorf and his friend Toby is Statler, though as far as I can tell it makes no odds. But they do make a great double act. I tried very hard not to be an overly proud parent, and I certainly refrained from posting on social media about it, but the two of them were genuinely funny. They had the whole room laughing. I could see Sam was trying to suppress his fatherly pride as well, while Karen was laughing louder than the whole room put together.

I was glad to have tickets to go again on the following night with Natalie and her mum Becky, although they were so full of compliments too it was almost embarrassing. Who am I kidding? It was brilliant!

Anyway, now the show is over and we've just got Holly's turn next week, on the very last day of term. Still young enough to be in the nativity plays, this year she is going to be a shepherd. She's already got her sights set on next year when she too will have graduated to doing the big kids' play, stating that the nativity is boring, and the same every year. She sees what Ben does and thinks she should be able to do exactly the same, neither age nor gender getting in the way. In fact, she has become increasingly keen on correcting any gender-stereotyping she encounters. "I am a shepherd not shepherdess," she corrected my dad.

"Oh, I'm sorry, I feel so sheepish," he had countered.

It had taken a moment, then, "Grandad!" she'd exclaimed, and Ben had murmured, "Tumbleweed," rolling his eyes.

"Look, Mr Big Time Comedian," Dad said to him, "I'm doing my best, OK? I've got a lot to live up to."

Ben had grinned, and he'd let Dad hug him. It's a rare thing these days, managing to have a hug with Ben, and I could tell he was only really tolerating this one, but it was good to see.

"I remember when your mum was a shepherde — shepherd," he corrected himself. "Fell off the stage, didn't you, Alice?"

"Oh yes, very funny."

"Did you, Mummy?"

"Yes, I was meant to be leading the shepherds off stage and I forgot where the steps were and I just walked straight through the curtain and fell to the floor. I hurt my ankle," I said, manifesting my infant self and still remembering my pain. Thankfully I was too young for it to have affected my reputation at school. In fact I suspect my classmates may not have given it a second thought, falling over or off things being par for the course for most four- or five-year-olds. Imagine doing that at secondary school… I'd have never lived it down. "Anyway, you weren't there, were you Dad?"

"No, that's true, that was the year the car got stuck…"

"Oh yes," Mum said, ruffling Dad's hair and looking at him fondly. "Poor old Alice, though."

"She wasn't old then," Ben said, the implication clear: 'but she is now'.

I do remember being upset about it, and my teacher being really kind, and Mum and Grandma coming backstage and whisking me home early, then being upset all over again when I realised Dad wasn't there and hadn't made it to my play.

Christmas does all sorts of funny things to us, not least exhausting us. Are we made to cope with all the hype? Not really, but still I love it. I used to love making people's Christmases special at the Sail Loft and then at Amethi, which I feel like I miss more and more as time goes on. Yet I probably feel ever-so-slightly less shattered than when I was trying to organise a bunch of strangers' Christmases as well as the family's.

This year, I have decided to put some of that

creativity into our own Christmas and go early, and big, on the decorations around the home. And Mum and Dad, having gone on a cruise last year and decided it's not for them – not at this time of year at least – are coming to us on Christmas Day, as well as Karen and Ron. We are going to have a nicely full house.

We will be missing Sophie again this year, and Janie and Jonathan and baby Joseph, who are enjoying their first family Christmas in Spain.

Sam is a bit put-out about Sophie staying in Devon again, but I get it. She is really too old now to have to alternate Christmases between her mum and dad.

"She's growing up," I have told Sam. "Maybe even grown up. She'll want to spend time with her old mates, I expect. They'll be back home from wherever they are these days."

"Yeah, but what about us? And Amber? She's her best friend."

"I know," I consoled him. "But she's seeing Amber at New Year, isn't she? And she'll want to see Harry I expect, on Christmas Day."

Harry and Sophie have been together for a while and, though I like him, Sam is not too keen. "He'll have her married and pregnant in two years if we're not careful," he has grumbled to me.

Though I can see what he means – Harry does seem a bit old before his time – I'm quite surprised by how protective Sam is towards his oldest daughter, and I am extremely glad he never found out about her pregnancy scare a few years back.

"He won't. And it's up to Sophie as well, you know. Girls are allowed to make their own minds up these days."

This elicited a wry smile from him.

"Look, Sophie's in a difficult position." I pressed my advantage. "She's been up and down between two homes, two parents, for a long time now. She's got younger – much younger – half-siblings, and she lost her job not long ago. It can't be easy. Let her do what's right for her, and she'll appreciate it. And then we'll have loads of fun together at New Year. OK?"

"OK," Sam had kissed me. "You're right."

"Well of course I am."

"But I kind of wish Kate and Isaac weren't going to be here too, at New Year."

"I know, but they're staying with his parents, aren't they? They'll be in Penzance most of the time. Sophie will be with us, we'll just all get together on New Year's Eve."

"I suppose."

Anyway, aside from little wobbles like that, all is shaping up nicely. And the house looks absolutely beautiful, if I do say so myself. Warm lights cascading down the front of it – classily, mind you – and a new wreath on the front door, made at a workshop I went to with Mum, Natalie and Becky.

Indoors, garlands adorn shelves and the staircase banister, with tiny twinkling lights intertwined. There are essential oil scents of oranges, cloves and ginger so that Sam says it smells like I'm drinking mulled wine all the time. And tomorrow – somehow I have managed to make us all wait till the weekend before Christmas for this – the pièce de rèsistance. The tree.

Lydia said we could have one from Amethi but that feels wrong. Instead, we're going with David and

Martin and Esme, who are having their first Christmas without Tyler (he's visiting his US girlfriend Macy, which is a story in itself), and so we're going tree-cutting with them, followed by a pub lunch, to try and cheer them up. It's going to be a tricky one for them this year, though an amazing experience for Tyler. He too will be back for New Year – along with Macy - but I do feel for them, and for Sam, missing Sophie. It's not the same for me, though I'd love to have Sophie here of course. But I have it all to come, I know, though we've hopefully got a few years yet before Ben and Holly want to be doing their own thing. But maybe that's what's pushing me on, to make each Christmas the best it can be, with all of the people I love around me for as long as possible.

1.

"So have you heard much from Tyler?" I ask David as Sam, Martin and Esme stride ahead with Ben and Holly.

"Not much," he says glumly. "He messaged to say he'd arrived. In fact he rang us from the airport when he was waiting for his *ride*, as he called it. What's wrong with *lift*, I ask you? Honestly, he's getting more American by the day. I think he was quite nervous though, bless him."

"I'm sure. It's a big deal, isn't it? Going to somebody else's family Christmas. And he's only met Macy once in person too – and he's so young!" I'm quite surprised that Martin and David have allowed Tyler to do this but they're keen to encourage his sense of adventure.

"I know," David says, pulling his coat about him. In contrast to last December, it is actually cold this year. The wind has an icy edge. "I think he's mad. Or maybe we are, not him. He's just in love. Although we both know that is a kind of madness in itself. I don't know. It's a lot for us oldies to get our heads round, isn't it? I mean, we'd just get drunk and meet somebody in a pub or a club. They'd either be local or on holiday. These guys meet online and I know they talk and talk and talk while they're gaming or whatever but is that really a basis for a relationship?"

"I know what you mean but it's the world that they know, isn't it? And really, is it any more realistic that you'll make a go of things with some random person you meet at a bar?"

"I certainly made a lot of bad decisions that way," David admits, smiling and looking like he doesn't really consider all of them bad decisions. "But – I don't know. I miss him, of course, but I'm worried about him too. Staying with some strangers. My fears run from them being crazy axe-murderers to religious fundamentalists who want to convert him and steal his passport so he can't come home, to him just realising he hasn't really got anything in common with Macy and being stuck with her and her family for the whole of Christmas."

"I can completely understand all of that. It must be very, very hard letting them go. Watching them make their own mistakes." I look wistfully towards my own two, who are racing each other along the woodland path, trying to get David and Martin's daughter to join in. She is resisting, walking instead with Sam and Martin. "I bet Esme's missing him too."

"Yeah, it'll be weird for her. But now she's met someone as well. Well, I think she has. She's certainly being quite mysterious and secretive about something and I can only assume it's a boy."

"Or a girl," I remind him.

"Oh yes, or a girl! Funny that even I am so ingrained with the classic hetero relationship assumption! But she's so young still. So that's something else to worry about."

"Stop!" I laugh, slipping my arm through David's. "It feels like you are actively looking to find things to stress about. Try and chill. It's Christmas. And look, we've got the party tonight."

"Oh yeah, well I am a little bit excited about that."

Lydia and Si Davey – I really need to start just thinking of him as Si, but it's hard when he's somebody I first knew of as a famous actor, always referred to by his full name – are having a Christmas party, at Amethi.

"It's a celebration of this year, Ivy coming to us, and her first Christmas, and… and just life really!" Lydia is so happy these days, it's just lovely. She suits motherhood very well indeed and I know she loves living at Amethi. On good days this makes it a bit easier that it's not mine and Julie's place anymore. On bad days I am just childishly jealous.

"So who's coming, that I'll know?" David asks.

"Me and Sam!" I laugh. "And then a whole bunch of celebrities."

"I won't know what to talk about," David says.

"I've never known that to be a problem for you before."

"Hey!" he nudges me. "I don't know what you mean."

"There will be a few other local types anyway. Your sister, for starters – and Paul and Shona of course – but that's about it for anyone local. I know Lydia invited Michael and his wife, and Cindy and Rod, but they've both cried off. I saw Cindy the other day and she said she just didn't feel like she'd fit in."

Michael supplies Amethi with all its dairy produce, and Cindy used to clean for me and Julie when we ran the place. Now she and her husband Rod work together in the kitchen there. With some advice from Julie, Cindy has trained as a chef, and she's excellent, but she says she feels very much like the employee, and is not at all at ease with the thought of hobnobbing with a load of stars.

David's sister Bea, however, my old boss and now slightly intimidating but lovely friend, will manage to fit right in. I wish I had half of her self-belief, though I know it's partially bravado. She can certainly carry it off anyway. "I'm hoping to meet a toy boy," she told me, only half-joking. Since Bob, the love of her life, died, Bea has not been in any serious relationships and says she has no intention of doing so: "But I'm not a nun, Alice!" she has told me more than once.

Lydia has outside caterers for tonight as this party is probably a step beyond what Cindy is prepared for and I know she had really hoped Cindy and Rod would come as guests. Once a waitress at the Sail Loft, she is still very much the daughter of a local family and I know she'd like a few more people from her world to be there tonight but I think a lot of people are scared off by the thought of trying to hold their own in a room of Bafta nominees and millionaires.

"They're just people," I told Cindy, really hoping to convince myself as well as make sure I've got another friend at the party who isn't an actor or director.

"Yeah, I know, and they're always really nice when they stay at Amethi but I just don't know… I'm old enough these days to realise I don't have to go to things if I don't feel comfortable about them. And we've got the family coming down the next day too. I'd just like to get ready for that." Cindy had shrugged.

"I get it," I'd said. And the thought of staying home tonight is increasingly attractive to me too, but I know Lydia is counting on us. Also, I've got Mum and Dad lined up for babysitting and I know Ben and Holly are looking forward to that just as much as they are. I do fantasize about Sam and I sneaking off and just having an evening together. A table for two at the Cross Section; a night in the pub; a walk on the beach. But there is no way we would get away with it. David would never forgive us, and neither would Lydia.

"Mum!" Holly shouts. "We've found it! We've found our tree!"

"Brilliant!" I call back, smiling at her excitement, and her beaming smile. "I'll be right there!"

Sam puts his hands on Holly's shoulders and smiles at me too and I feel a little rush of love.

I squeeze David's arm as we approach. "We'll have a great time tonight, and you'll have a lovely Christmas. I'm sure Tyler will too. And you can host Macy next year!"

"Oh my god," he groans.

I laugh as we reach our little group and the nursery worker approaches, Ben pointing out 'our tree' to him.

"Isn't it beautiful?" Holly asks.

"It really is," I say, swallowing back my feeling of guilt as we choose this lovely, unsuspecting tree, only for it to be sawn down and laid on the back of the nursery worker's truck. *We'll make you beautiful,* I find myself trying to tell it via the power of thought, though I am not sure the tree would really appreciate being smothered by baubles, lights and tinsel, or consider it a fair price for its life.

Once Martin and Esme have pointed out their tree and that too has been cut down in its prime, we continue on the circular walk, enjoying the chill of the air and the melody of the robin that flits from tree to tree, accompanying us along the route. From deeper into the woodland comes more resonant birdsong and I imagine other creatures in there too; foxes, badgers, mice… tucked into their warm homes, safe from prying eyes, biding their time until twilight comes and they can emerge into the sanctuary of the darker hours.

Esme plays hide and seek with Ben and Holly, pretending not to be able to find my daughter, whose sense of her own size seems to have stopped at the age of about four so that she still thinks she can be obscured by a spindly bush.

"Have you seen Holly anywhere?" Esme asks us.

"No, I don't think so," I say, pretending not to hear the giggling of my child.

Ben, meanwhile, seems to have genuinely vanished, and I have to repress a very primal sense of fear. While Holly can't suppress her laughter or her urge to show Esme her "really great" hiding place, it does genuinely take a couple of minutes to find Ben, who has insinuated himself into a large tree stump.

"Bloody hell Ben!" Sam says, and I see he too may have been experiencing that same slight anguish, even though we knew it was just a game. With Holly's diabetes we sometimes feel we are teetering on the edge of safety with her and I think that has leaked into other areas of our life. I mean, it's fine. Holly is fine – and fit and healthy – but it's just that constant unease, which never really goes away. That knowledge that we rely on her pump, and of course a regular supply of insulin, to keep her well, keep her living. And sometimes like we are just a step or two from the precipice. How easily and quickly something could go wrong. It does make you look at life a little bit differently.

But Ben is fine, and Holly is fine. I tell myself this and we press on, and by the time we've reached the parking area again there are two netted trees ready for us, which Martin and David load into the back of their van.

Now their children are older, they've invested in this lovely little van and take off at weekends, sometimes up country, visiting old friends and sometimes just to the coast, or up to the moors, camping out overnight and enjoying their freedom. I must admit, that is one of the more enticing thoughts about the children growing up and every now and then I think it will be just me and Sam again. My stomach contracts at the thought of not having Ben and Holly with us in our everyday lives but equally there's a slight sense of something exciting, having time for the two of us again. But that is a long way off yet. Even so, even before then, will come a time when our children are better able to fend for themselves, and we might find a bit more freedom.

For now though, I am just so grateful to have Mum and Dad, and Karen and Ron, around, to give us a night off every once in a while. Like tonight, in fact – and again I imagine saying to Sam, let's forget the party and go out, just you and me. He'd be up for it. He's already uncomfortable at the thought of his tuxedo, and having to chat to a load of snotty celebs as he can't help but think of them, though he really likes Lydia and Si and we both know they won't have awful friends. At least I hope not. I try to quell the nerves in my stomach.

They're just people, I tell myself, as I'd told Cindy. Even so, I feel a little twist of unease in my gut.

With the trees safely stowed away in the van, at Holly's request Esme comes with us in our car and we set off for lunch. As we did last year, we're having a pre-Christmas meal at the Three Barrels, a lovely little pub just outside town. As we step through the low doorway, Sam and Martin having to stoop a little to avoid banging their heads, the warmth of the fire and the conversation draw us in, wrap themselves around us.

Amber, Sophie's friend, looks up from pulling a pint and smiles.

"Hi guys!"

"Hi Amber," I say, going straight to the bar, Esme by my side. "Happy Christmas!"

"And the same to you. Sophie said you were out looking for trees this morning. Did you find any?" She looks to Esme.

"There were a few," David and Martin's daughter grins. "In the woods, at least."

"Makes sense," Amber grins back. "Let me get this pint to that gentleman over there and I'll be right with you."

"Thanks, Amber. What are you having, Esme?"

"No, no, I'll get these," she insists.

"You can't do that! There's all four of us, and your dads…"

"Honestly, it's fine, we can work it out later."

When did she get so grown up? I feel like she's older than her years sometimes. David and Martin allow her and Tyler a lot of freedom – and not at all in a way that suggests they don't care. They just trust them. Hence Tyler's Christmas in the States, though I do get the feeling David's doubting that decision.

Esme is working at a local hotel, which is of course something I know all about, but she's still studying too and I think she is burning the candle at both ends. But David tells me she's doing really well at work and not bothered about further education. Both he and Martin want her to make her own mind up. And I can't help but think of Lydia, who was much the same as Esme, and look at her now. I only hope I can be so trusting with Ben and Holly when they're older but I suspect I'm going to find it harder to step back if I think they're making a mistake.

Mature though she may be, Esme is not old enough to be legally buying alcohol so I stay by her side but agree to let her pay.

"That's very kind of you Esme, thank you. I'll have a lime and soda, Sam will have a half of pale ale, and the kids will have Fruit Shoots please." I try and choose the least expensive drinks and, once the order's in I say, "Let me know if you need a hand carrying them."

I go over to the table. "Esme's insisted on paying for the drinks," I say, looking over to the bar where she and Amber are laughing about something.

"Well she wants to," Martin says proudly. "It makes her feel good. She's growing up fast and she's loving working and earning her own money. I say we let her. David and I will make sure she's alright anyway."

"OK," I say, and I notice when Esme comes over that she's bought Sam a pint, not a half. She sees me looking and shrugs. "It's Christmas, isn't it?"

When we all have our drinks and are seated, I raise a toast. "To friends and family, and to Esme for buying the drinks!"

"To Esme!" everyone at the table says, and Amber echoes the same from behind the bar. Esme turns briefly and grins, her cheeks flushed. Then, to deflect any further attention, she picks up her menu. "What's everyone having?"

"You're not getting this as well are you, Esme?" Sam asks and she looks up, panicked. He smiles, kindly. "Just kidding! Thanks very much for the pint though."

"You're welcome."

"I'm having the turkey dinner with the works," David announces.

"We're eating out tonight, David!" Martin admonishes. "Don't you want to save yourself for that?"

"It's too late to save myself," David grins. "Anyway, I had a run this morning, just so I could have two dinners today."

"That's not really how it's meant to work." Martin rolls his eyes. "It'll catch up with you one day, you know. I think I'll have the goat's cheese and beetroot salad."

"Urgh!" Holly proclaims.

"Holly!" I say, but Martin is laughing.

"I agree, it sounds awful!"

When Amber comes to take our orders, Sam asks if she's heard from Sophie.

"Yeah, we're planning our outfits. For New Year, I mean."

"And what are you going as?"

"Nice try, Sophie's dad! You know she'll kill me if I tell you!"

Whenever Sophie spends New Year in Cornwall, she and Amber make it a point of pride to surprise us with their fancy dress. They've been Ginger Spice (Amber) and Sporty Spice (Sophie); Ant and Dec; a pair of mermaids, and, most recently, the Pet Shop Boys – Sophie had a makeshift keyboard suspended around her neck, which was quite a cunning idea, made as it was from a tray so she and Amber could rest their drinks on it. Unfortunately it all went a bit wrong when a bunch of their school friends tried to do the same and the strap snapped, sending glasses and bottles plummeting and drinks sinking into the cold, wet sand of the harbour beach.

"Fine, I won't tell you what I'm going as."

"I'm not that fussed, to be honest." Amber grins cheekily and Esme laughs.

"That's enough cackling from you two!" David says. "Honestly, young people today. Now, Amber, I'll have the Christmas dinner with all the trimmings please."

"Aren't you at the party tonight?" Amber – who also works as a waitress at Amethi when required – asks.

"Don't you start!" says David, and Holly, feeling flushed and excited, shouts "Greedy David!"

She is gratified by more laughter from the bigger girls but I feel the need to tell her not to be cheeky.

"Takes after her mum," David says.

"I shan't be sticking up for you again then," I say. "Greedy David."

Amber takes all our orders, including another pint for Sam. I raise my eyebrows at him.

"It's Christmas, isn't it?" he asks, repeating Esme's words, and I am just happy to see him looking so relaxed. In fact, we are all in great spirits. And this afternoon, we get to put the tree up and decorate it.

I can sense Holly's excitement bubbling up and frothing over and I can't help but catch a bit of it myself. My own childhood Christmases may be a very long time ago now but I still remember them, and how it feels, to be wrapped up in the warmth and the magic of not just Christmas but all that time with family and friends, and visiting grandparents, aunts, uncles and cousins, the hard work of preparing for Christmas over and now allowed to just stop and enjoy each other, away from the stresses and strains of the outside world for a few precious days.

2.

Predictably, the two lunchtime pints have Sam taking a little afternoon nap. Long gone are those daytime drinking days, when we had the time – and disposable income – to spend the occasional afternoon in a pub, extending on into the evening with a party on the beach or at somebody's house, sometimes getting up early for work the next day feeling tired and maybe having a bit of a headache but not much more worse for wear than that.

"When are we doing the tree?" Holly wails. "Can't you wake Daddy up?"

"Just give him half an hour," I say, keen to make sure Sam's on good form for the party tonight as well.

"That's ages!" she complains.

"It's not, not really. Look, we can get the decorations out, untangle the lights, check they're working, and by the time we've done that Daddy will be awake. If he's not I'll take him a cup of tea and wake him up, OK?"

"That's boring," she says.

I suppress a sigh. "OK, I'll get the decorations out, you can watch *Stick Man*. Alright? That's half an hour and then it will be time for Daddy to wake up."

"Fine," she huffs, offering me a vision of a future, teenage Holly, and she flounces onto the settee, putting her arm out for Poppy to join her, which she duly does. And, TV on, Holly allows herself to relax for a while, transfixed by Julia Donaldson's story, even though she will never let me read this to her these days – or *The Gruffalo*. I already miss those picture-book days but she does at least still like me or Sam to read to her at bedtime and even Ben does, so we're hanging on in there with those 'little' times, and I'm planning to make them last as long as I possibly can.

"Urgh, my head hurts," grumbles Sam as I wake him up with a not-too-delicate placing of a mug of tea on his bedside table.

"There's a paracetamol there too," I tell him.

"You're an angel," he says, curling his arm around my waist and attempting to pull me towards him.

"I am, it's true. But we have a tree to decorate, I'm afraid. And a little girl about to burst with frustration." I extricate myself gently, edging away from him.

"Oh… yeah."

"And a party to go to."

"Oh yeah." This said with a distinct lack of enthusiasm.

I glance at his tux hanging on the outside of the wardrobe. My dress next to it. We are neither of us dressing-up types but I am kind of excited at the sight. Even so, I feel like we're going to stick out like sore thumbs tonight, amongst the designer dresses and suits, and I'm glad that we will have Martin and David as fellow bumpkins, though they are far more stylish than either of us.

"It'll be fun!" I say, trying to convince us both. "Now

come on please, I can't contain Holly for much longer. I'll go and tell Ben too."

"OK," Sam says, pulling himself up. "Whose idea was it to have two pints at lunchtime anyway?"

"I'm pretty sure it was yours."

"Oh. Yeah."

In another ten minutes, a fairly presentable Sam makes an appearance, Ben hot on his heels.

"I'll just make another cup of tea," Sam says.

"No, Daddy!" Holly protests. "We've already waited ages for you."

"OK," he concedes, picking her up and swinging her into the air. "Seeing as it's you."

She giggles and he hugs her to him.

And once the lights are on, swirled around the tree and tucked into the recesses of its branches, we let the kids loose with the baubles, strings of beads and tinsel, and Sam sneaks into the kitchen to make some coffee, Holly so intent on her creativity that she doesn't even notice.

He brings a tray in and we sit down together, Sam leaning back with his arm around me and Poppy, always so touchingly desperate for affection, pushing herself into my other side. I close my eyes for a few moments, enjoying Sam's reassuring presence, the warm urgency of Poppy, nudging my hand to keep me rubbing her fur, and listening to the voices of my children as they decide what should go where on the tree.

And I, like Sam, must have been in need of a nap because the next thing I'm aware of is Holly shouting, "Wake up, Mummy, the tree's ready!"

I snap to attention. "Was I snoring?"

"Yes!" Ben laughs.

I look at Sam.

"A little bit," he smiles.

Damn.

"Are we ready for the big switch-on then?" I ask, immediately back in the swing of things. I gently move Poppy away so I can stand up, and take a big swig of my coffee, which is lukewarm so maybe I really did have a good few minutes' sleep. Anyway, I feel good, and I go to the patio doors to pull the floor-length curtains closed, while Sam does the ones at the front of the house. The room is in near darkness and we count down from ten to one, and then Sam switches on the lights and the four of us draw together, arms around each other, Poppy pushing herself in between Ben and Holly, all of us admiring the messy splendour of the tree.

"What a beauty!" Dad exclaims when he and Mum arrive, late afternoon. I know enough by now to have realised that if they didn't come till later in the day – half an hour before we go out, for example – I will be too busy with Ben and Holly (particularly Holly) to have time to really get myself ready. And you know what I mean about getting ready: I will need to try that dress on, have my doubts about it, try something else on just in case, then put the original dress back on again, and do my hair and make-up. I'm not even somebody who is that bothered about these things, but I suffer from last-minute self-doubt and particularly when faced with the prospect of a room full of glamorous people from the world of film and TV. I know, they're just people. I know that. I also know it doesn't matter what I look like – what anyone looks like. That appearance is pretty much the least important thing about anyone. And yet… I still want to go out feeling confident and that I look good. It's sad but it's true.

I don't want to feel like Lydia and Si's friends will look down on us, and I already suspect that I might be out of my depth. We really do live in different worlds, and I can feel myself becoming defensive at the imagined slights we are about to suffer. I know, I know, I'm the one with the preconceptions, and I am sure that we're going to have a lovely evening. I suppose I am just feeling the nerves.

Breathe, Alice. Lizzie's words float into my mind as they often do when I'm feeling unsure of myself. *Be in the moment.*

And the moment is this: Holly shouting "Grandad!" and leaping into his arms, nearly knocking him flying.

"Hello little Christmas leaf," he says, laughing.

"Careful, Holly," Mum says half-seriously. "Grandad's not as young as he used to be."

"And you're not as little as you used to be!" Dad says to my daughter, placing her down so she is standing on the settee and then sitting down next to her, wincing as she begins to bounce up and down. "I wish I had half your energy, little leaf."

"I'm not a leaf!" she shrieks, laughing.

"You are, you're a little prickly holly! You know there's a carol about you, don't you? And it's Cornish!"

Dad sings a few lines from the Carol of Saint Day:

"And the first tree in the greenwood, it was the holly.

The holly, the holly.

Oh, the first tree in the greenwood, it was the holly."

"Grandad! You can't sing!" Holly shrieks.

He grabs her and begins tickling her till she is almost breathless and Mum has to reprimand him instead.

"Phil! You two are as bad as each other."

"Life's too short to be boring eh, Holly?" Dad says, nudging his granddaughter, who leans happily into him.

"Mum, will you be OK looking after three kids tonight?" I ask.

"I don't need looking after," Ben announces, striding into the room. "Hi Grandma, hi Grandad." He allows himself to be kissed by Mum, who shoots me a knowing look.

I just smile and shrug. This is Ben. He's growing up.

"Cup of tea?" I ask, and Mum follows me into the kitchen.

"Everything OK?" I ask, noticing she looks a bit tired.

"Oh, yeah, I just feel a bit coldy. And your dad didn't sleep well last night, so I didn't either."

"Are you sure you're OK to babysit?" I ask, a tiny part of me looking for an excuse to cry off from tonight. I do want to go. But I don't. It would be so much easier to just stay at home. And now the tree is decorated, the temptation of a cosy evening in is very strong.

"We'll be fine," Mum says. "You and Sam go and enjoy yourselves."

"Alright," I say, accepting my fate. "Well, there's tea

for all of you in the fridge, and the carb count of course–" Mum is great at Holly's diabetes care and it's a relief to have somebody else who knows what's what – "and the kids want to watch a movie with you, though they can't agree which one, so you might have to do some refereeing—"

"We will be fine, Alice," Mum assures me, putting her hand on my arm. "Now, are you putting that kettle on or not?"

3.

"You look so good," Sam says, kissing the nape of my neck as he slips my necklace around it then does up the clasp. A tiny ripple of goose pimples travels down my back, like a spring breeze rippling the surface of the sea.

I look at myself in the mirror, not quite sure it's me I'm looking at, wearing a long dark green dress, with a small slit up the right side, as far as the knee. It's high chested; I am no longer in the habit of displaying my cleavage to anyone, and it is very flatteringly fitted. Here, in our bedroom, I feel ridiculously overdressed, but I know I will almost certainly feel the opposite this evening. Still, I will have to do. *Personality over appearance, Alice,* I tell myself.

I know will be OK. I can normally make conversation with anyone, it just takes a bit of extra energy sometimes. I am very glad that we have a quiet day tomorrow.

"You also look quite good," I say, pulling Sam gently round to my side so we can look at each other in the mirror. "In fact, we make quite a nice-looking pair," I say, so glad Sam is not the type to make a quip about me having a *nice pair. Tee hee.*

"We scrub up pretty well," he says, "though maybe I should have a shave." He rubs his chin.

"No, don't shave just for tonight. Half of them will probably have moustaches anyway."

"True. And mullets?"

"The younger ones, maybe," I say, not really having any clue what might be en vogue for the people we're going to be mixing with.

"Should we eat something before we go?"

"I don't think I can," I say, placing my hand flat on my not-flat stomach and feeling a sharp stab of nerves in my gut.

"We should have something. It might be all canapés and small plates," Sam says, rolling his eyes. I know he's feeling a little bit like me; unsure of himself and not really confident about the evening. The pre-emptive criticisms are a form of defence.

"It'll be lovely," I say with more confidence than I feel. "And Lydia and Si will have made sure there's loads of great food. But maybe you do want to soak up the lunchtime's beer."

"I'll just have an egg butty," Sam says.

"OK," I say, images of his crisp white (hired) shirt streaked with bright orange yolk.

"I'll wear a bib, don't worry." Sam grins at me in the mirror and I nudge him then turn and snake my arms around his neck.

"We'll have a good time," I say, convincing neither of us. "And it's just one night anyway."

"It'll be fine, Alice." Sam has taken on the role of reassuring now. "We'll be fine. We'll be together, won't we? And if it's awful we can sneak outside and snog in the bird hide."

"It's a deal." I smile and kiss him.

He kisses me back. I feel the warmth of his lips, his familiar taste, though his breath is tinged slightly with the lunchtime's beer and the afternoon's sleep. "Maybe brush your teeth after your egg sarnie?" I suggest.

"And they say romance is dead."

"Oh my god, look at you two!" Julie exclaims, beaming onto our TV screen all the way from Canada. We've set up the camera so she can see all of us and the tree. "Turn around Alice," she commands, and I do.

Luke emits a low whistle. "Looking good there, and you too, Sammy. You look like…"

"Don't say James Bond," interrupts Sam.

"I was going to say Mr Bean."

A loud laugh erupts from Dad.

"Stand up, Julie," I say to my friend. "Maybe you can do a twirl for us too."

She obliges, standing slowly, and her bump emerges from below the surface of the desk. "I can't believe you're making a heavily pregnant geriatric mother do this," she smiles. I smile too. I can see how much she loves being pregnant. It's tough for her because, having adopted Zinnia, she does not want her daughter to feel any less special because she wasn't conceived naturally – yet at the same time Julie was so shocked to be pregnant after all those years of trying, and is clearly so delighted with the experience. Geriatric she may be in medical terms, but she looks incredible. I tell her so.

"It's not quite your slinky green dress," she says ruefully, looking down at her high-waisted maternity joggers.

"You look beautiful, Julie," Dad says.

"You really do," agrees Mum.

"When are you having the baby?" Holly calls out, then buries her head in Dad's arm, suddenly shy.

"Very soon, I hope!" Julie laughs. "How are you, Holly? I believe it's your birthday very soon. How old are you going to be? Twenty-seven?"

"No! Seven!" Holly shouts.

"Seven? You can't be seven!"

"I am going to be seven."

"Well that is just crazy," Julie says, and I know she is looking at me, and if I'm not much mistaken her eyes are shining. It's hard, trying to convey something via a screen, especially with my family around me, and Luke next to her, but I think I manage it. She gets it, how extraordinarily grateful I am for Holly being alive and well and growing as she should – and I get it, how extraordinarily grateful she is for this baby which is due imminently. And how once upon a time we were just two kids, with no idea whatsoever of how our lives would play out. I feel another sharp twist inside me, this time at thought of how much I miss my friend.

"And who is that young lady behind you?" Dad breaks the spell, and I notice Zinnia has drifted into view. She is wearing a hoodie and has some pretty nice-looking headphones around her neck.

"Zinnia!" Holly shouts, her shyness forgotten. Even Ben perks up.

"Shall we leave the kids to it?" I ask. "We're going to have to get going soon anyway."

"Call me tomorrow Alice, I want to know all the showbiz goss," Julie says.

"Of course! Though I think you'll be disappointed. But I'll definitely call anyway." I want to speak to her every day, make sure she's OK, and – if I'm honest – I want to be part of her baby's birth in some small way. I find myself daydreaming that her waters will break while I'm on a call with her. That she'll keep me connected on her way to the hospital and into the delivery room. *It's not about you, Alice,* I have to remind myself over again. I suppose I just want to miss out on such a huge thing in Julie's life but I can't really expect to be the first thing on her mind. And she is in Canada and I am here. Best friends for life and the closest thing to sisters but as she said to me when she told me about their plans to leave Cornwall, our priorities are our families these days, and that's exactly as it should be. I just miss her.

At 7pm prompt, a car horn sounds outside and Sam and I look at each other. "Guess it's time to go."

Holly has already run through her list of possible reasons that we shouldn't leave her and Ben, even though she's with Mum and Dad and will be absolutely fine, and she knows it. I think she is just going through something like separation anxiety and would rather we were all together.

I've got a tummy ache/headache/sore throat… I feel sick…

I have gently responded to all of these complaints with reassurance that Mum and Dad will look after her if she needs anything, and that I am only a phone call away. And it is hard, leaving her. Diabetes is never far from my mind but also now we have had time to live with it I know we can deal with it, manage it, as long as we are on the case. And Mum will know what to do in the first instance and if she doesn't, she will call me. It means I can't ever switch off properly but these days I am better able to relax a little, and I am strict with myself about how often I check the app on my phone to see what Holly's blood glucose level is. We are so lucky to be able to do this, and it can be a real reassurance that all is OK, but tonight Mum or Dad will call if there's a problem.

I hug my son and daughter now but the pair of them are already wrapped up in something on TV and barely even look at me.

"*Have a nice time, Mummy,*" I mutter, rolling my eyes at Mum, who laughs.

"Have a *great* time," she says, kissing me and hugging Sam.

"Don't forget us mere mortals, will you?" Dad smiles. He slips a twenty-pound note into my hand. "Get yourselves a drink with this, OK?"

"Thanks, Dad." I don't tell him that Si and Lydia have laid on a fully-paid up bar and that these days most places are cashless anyway. I hug him tightly. "Have a nice time with the kids. And don't overdo it. Mum said you had a bad night's sleep."

"Oh yeah, but I had a power nap before we came here. I'll be right as rain. It's your mum who needs to rest, she's playing down this cold you know."

Selfishly, a little thought plays through my head, that I hope we don't all get Mum's cold, just in time for Christmas. I push it away.

"You'd better look after her then!" I smile. "Mum, Dad's going to wait on you hand and foot, OK?"

"Oh, well, I suppose, if he has to…"

"We won't be late anyway," Sam says.

"Just go out and enjoy yourselves, and stay as late as you want. We will be fine," Dad says firmly.

"Alright. Thank you."

I open the door, pulling my wrap around me as the winter air presses itself onto my bare skin.

"Look at you two!" I exclaim at the sight of Martin and David, who have both emerged from their car.

"So handsome!" Mum exclaims. "Let's get a photo of the four of you."

"Where's the red carpet?" asks David, mock-flouncing along the path.

"Ah yes, sorry, it's at the dry cleaners," I say, kissing him.

We line up in front of the Christmas lights, then Dad tells us to move as we just look like silhouettes, and we all shuffle along so that the backdrop is now the street, the neighbours' lights creating a suitably festive backdrop.

"Great, great. All say 'Merry Christmas!'" instructs Dad, and we do as we are told. "Lovely."

"Let's get one of you now, Phil," David says.

"Oh, really? OK," Dad says, handing his phone over, apparently unaware that David was joking.

"Dad!" I laugh, and I put my arm through his, pulling him to me and kissing his cold cheek.

"Perfect!" David says, snapping a few shots. "You get in them as well, Sue. You're too beautiful to stay out of shot."

Mum giggles slightly, as she often does with David.

Standing between my parents, I put my arms around their shoulders, taller than them both these days.

"Three… two… one…" David calls. "Merry Griffiths! Sam, are you going to step in?"

"I think that's quite enough photos," says Sam who, though not really keen on this party, also does not like to be late for anything. "Come on."

"Alright! Anyway, you two should get back in the warm," I say to Mum and Dad. "Call me if there's any problems."

"There won't be," Mum says, pulling a tissue out of her sleeve to blow her nose. "But we will."

And then we are climbing into David's car, which is pristine and still smells new, even though he's had it for months, and I watch Mum and Dad go into our house, a small part of me wishing I was following them in, but then we are off – to a party none of us are sure about, but at least we are all together.

4.

"Oh wow!" Martin says as we glide along the once-bumpy drive up to Amethi, now as smooth as my silky dress and flanked at the entrance by two glittering trees, then festooned all the way along by chains of fairy lights on either side. In the field to the left graze some lit-up reindeer and it looks from here as if every tree has been decorated, and celebrated, with its own set of multi-coloured lights.

"It's just like Center Parcs," David breathes, which makes us all laugh.

It does look fantastic, though I have to work hard to push down that internal mini-Alice who tuts and thinks 'I wouldn't have done it like that.' It's a hard thing, letting go of the feeling of ownership. This place will always be mine and Julie's in my mind, but it isn't now. It is Lydia's, and Si's and Ivy's. It's their home; their refuge, as well as Lydia's business. And they are doing it proud.

I breathe deeply to try and calm my nerves, which does not go unnoticed by Sam. He looks across and offers a small smile, squeezing my hand though I know he is not feeling 100% comfortable himself. David pulls his perfectly nice newish electric car up next to some sporty number that all three of them seem to think is fantastic but which I have no clue about, and no wish to change that situation.

"Come on then," David turns to us. "Bumpkins assemble!"

We emerge from the car and I am emboldened by a sense of togetherness. I lead the way around the corner, where I am gratified to see that Lydia has kept the same place we always had for the large outdoor Christmas tree, and the same old lights adorn the accommodation, rising and falling like waves all along the old buildings.

"Can I have your phone?" I ask Sam. "I can keep it in my bag."

"Do you even need to have your bag?" he asks. "I could have your phone instead, keep them both in my pockets."

"I'd rather have them on me," I say. I know it's stupid but I will relax better if I do have my phone to hand – and Sam's as back-up. The signal up here can be a bit patchy so I know Mum will try me first if there's a problem, and then Sam if she can't get hold of me. I hope she doesn't have to but if I have the phones and they don't ring I will know I can relax. Well, I could if I wasn't going to be in a room full of TV and film stars.

I take Sam's hand as we round the corner to the Mowhay, and see that the firepit outside – around which Julie, Lizzie and I have hosted many a solstice and equinox celebration – is burning bright and keeping a couple of smokers warm as they enjoy their illicit cigarettes. The smells of the two types of smoke mingle as they reach our nostrils. I can't make out who those two figures are and they pay us no attention so I walk as best as I can across the gravel in my low-heeled shoes, to the entrance, where we are greeted by none other than Amber, dressed now in smart white shirt, black trousers and apron.

"Thank God you're here!" she says, kissing me. "This is so weird! Seeing all these people in real life."

She hands us small tin flagons of mulled wine, asking if we want alcoholic or non-alcoholic. "There's a lot of non-alcoholics here," she tells us.

"Or recovering alcoholics, more likely," David says a tad too loudly but it's not meant in judgement; he has had his fair share of drink-related issues.

Still, Martin hushes him and accepts his little flagon. "Love this cup!" he says.

"It's representative of the Cornish tin industry or something," Amber grins.

"Of course it is."

"And are the canapés tiny Cornish pasties?" asks Sam, which makes Amber giggle nervously, as she gestures to a fellow waitress who is indeed bearing a tray of tiny, perfectly formed pasties.

We all hold back our mirth.

"We're celebrating a Kernow Christmas," Amber says. "Look."

On the wall of the Mowhay is a beautiful, hand-painted banner bearing the words 'Nadelik Lowen'.

"Alice!" I feel a hand on my shoulder and turn to see Lydia. "I see you've noticed the Cornish theme," she says, rolling her eyes slightly. "I tried to put him off but Si was insistent that we show all these Londoners what they're missing. Even though half of them have been to stay here before, or else have their own second or third homes in Cornwall. And even though we absolutely, definitely do not subsist on pasties and cream teas."

I see a waiter pass by with a tray of tiny scones.

"Try one," Lydia says. "They're savoury, with cream cheese and chilli jam."

"Alright," I say. "Thank you. And the place looks beautiful."

"Do you think?" Her eyes seek mine, touchingly looking for approval. Part of it is her slight sense of guilt that Amethi is now hers, though I much prefer that to some stranger coming in and taking over – and part of it is still that slight feeling of me having been her manager and, as she sometimes tells me, a role model. I always laugh it off when she says that, though of course I kind of love it. Flattery will get you everywhere.

"Lydia, it is fantastic. And this scone is absolutely delicious," I say, spraying crumbs from my mouth and hoping nobody has noticed.

They're just people, I say those words again, in my head. They burp, fart, and use the loo just like everyone else. But oh, these women are so finely manicured and I imagine pedicured too, and their hair and make-up is perfect. Many of them are just this side of painfully thin, and poised and elegant. The men, too, all handsome in their black tie and coiffed hair. I can't imagine any of them with a crumb on them or dribbling mulled wine down their chin as I am paranoid about doing.

No mullets here either; the men are sporting beards or stubble, I'm pleased to see, so Sam will fit in nicely. I suppose I could be biased, but he is just as handsome and rugged as any of them.

"Paul and Shona are over there," Lydia says, "and

Bea too." I look across to a table where Shona is deep in conversation with… oh my god, is that Josh Craven? One of Si's co-stars in the recent British noir he starred in. Bea, meanwhile, is chatting to an older, distinguished-looking man (good work, Bea though I see the idea of a toy boy's gone out of the window) and Paul, having spotted us, is waving us over eagerly.

"Thank God you're here!" he says, echoing Amber's words. I am pleased to see him; we have another comrade, and it feels like we are all forming a little sub-layer of local folk, which I realise makes me sound horribly parochial.

"You look gorgeous," Paul says, pulling me towards him and kissing me on the cheek, his stubble grazing my skin and his subtle aftershave floating into my airways. He looks at Sam. "You look gorgeous too," he says, shaking his hand, and putting us both better at ease.

Paul looks effortlessly stylish in his tux, which definitely will not be hired, and Shona – who has not yet noticed us, being too engrossed in conversation with Josh – is looking fantastic. If I knew about fashion designers I'd be able to tell you who she is wearing but instead I can just tell you she is in a shortish black shift dress which looks both simple and incredibly sophisticated at the same time. She has black heels on too, and diamonds in her ears and around her neck, matching the extremely large diamond in the engagement ring Paul gave her.

I remember how these two got married, taking Sam's and my place at the longhouse after Sam had his accident. And how at one time, long before that, I'd wondered if Paul and I could have had a future together. It's a crazy thought to me now, we are poles apart, but I still feel very fond of him.

"She's schmoozing," he says, "and I just have to sit here and look pretty."

"Well you're doing a great job," David interjects.

"Excuse my husband." Martin smiles at Paul, shaking his hand.

"Hey, I'll take compliments where I can get them these days," says Paul. "Sorry David, that doesn't sound very flattering to you."

"None taken," David says. He pulls out a chair, offering it to me. "My lady?"

I am grateful to sit down, sink into the background, trying not to look or feel awed by the famous faces here.

"There's a table plan," Paul says.

"Oh no, is there?" A flurry of fear beats in my chest, like a bat is trapped there and trying to get out.

"Yes, but it's OK, we're all together."

I am relieved, and grateful to Si and Lydia. While I don't want to be cast as the outsiders – locals brought in to make up the numbers – and I do want to be somebody who can hold their own in any company, what would I really find to talk to these people about?

Lydia, though the graceful hostess, also seems to appreciate having a small group of non-celebs to hang out with, and she spends as much time with us as she can, between regular apologetic interjections from Si, who whisks her off to speak with various individuals.

"I'll be glad when I can just get back to Ivy," she tells me.

"Who's got her now?"

"Her uncles! She's in her element."

When Lydia worked for me, her younger brothers were still at school and she spent quite a lot of time helping to look after them, between shifts at the Sail Loft and studying. Now, it seems, they are paying her back, and from what I've seen they are neither impressed nor awed by Si's celebrity status.

"Wouldn't they have liked to come to this?" I ask. "Look at these beautiful women!"

"No, I gave them the option but they're not fussed. They'd rather look after Ivy. They're both besotted."

"I don't blame them. She's even more beautiful. But make the most of tonight, won't you? I can see how much you've put into it. And I know you already know this but they're just people." I can't help myself, trying to sound like I'm totally fine with it all and still a little bit older and wiser than Lydia. "Who am I kidding?" I admit, ruefully. "I'm bloody terrified of them!"

"I'm just grateful you're here Alice, and they're alright really, most of them. Si wouldn't have invited the dickheads. Well maybe one or two, to keep them on side, but I'll try and point them out to you. Apart from them, they're nice. They're just people."

She grins and I laugh.

"Wise words, Lydia. Wise words."

As it happens, it's a nice evening. Si gives a little speech toasting Ivy, and Lydia, and singing the praises of Cornish life. There is a set by the local shanty singers, which takes me back to the party we threw for Luke and Julie's anniversary, bringing a few tears to my eyes. I wipe them away but not before David has noticed.

Dinner, thankfully, swerves away from the 'Cornish' theme, although everything has been sourced, grown, caught, bred or baked locally. For us vegetarians there is the most delicious nut roast I have ever had, punctured with sweet apricots, and accompanied by seasonal vegetables and Cornish puddings (Yorkshire puddings with Saffron added in honour of the Cornish Saffron buns). Every mouthful is delicious, and Sam needn't have worried about small plates or being hungry. The wine is flowing and there are cheese boards for every table, as well as cheesecake or profiteroles (or both), twinkling with gold leaf decoration, and gorgeous coffee and hand-crafted chocolate mints to follow. Soon I'm absolutely stuffed.

"How you are you doing there, David?" I grin at my friend, seeing even he looks slightly defeated by the sheer volume of rich, delicious food.

As all the plates are cleared away, we are asked to stand for a while and even encouraged to go outside and admire the peace and the star-strewn sky while the caterers rearrange the tables and chairs, and a small dancefloor is created.

Amid the bustle of people heading out of the door, I am forced into conversation with a woman who, though I have never met her before, is incredibly familiar-looking. She is very pleasant and asks my name.

"Not *the* Alice?" she exclaims.

"Oh, er, erm…"

"You started this place up?"

"Oh, well, yes, with my friend Julie."

"Oh my god, yes, Julie! I've heard so much about you both, I feel like I know you."

I can't help smiling at this. Especially as I quickly realise where I know her from; a long-running detective series which I haven't actually watched but which is probably on its third or fourth series and has glowing reviews.

"I try and keep a low profile," I grin and am rewarded by an outburst of laughter.

"Oh yes, I don't blame you. Well, Si and Lydia both think the world of you, and I love this place. I love sneaking off here for some peace, though I haven't been here in the winter before. It's beautiful. So what are you doing now?"

"I'm being a mum," I say then add, quickly, not wanting her to think me boring or letting the side down. "And, actually, working with Shona. Si's agent."

"Oh my god, I love Shona too. So, that's interesting. Do you have a card? I might be in touch in the new year."

"I… don't. Not on me," I say, knowing full well I don't have a card at all, anywhere.

"That's OK, that's OK, I'll get your number from Si."

"Or maybe go through Shona?"

"Yes of course, either way. Catriona, by the way." She thrusts her hand towards me. I like the fact she introduces herself as if I wouldn't know who she is.

"Lovely to meet you," I say and, as she turns to wander off elsewhere I call, "Happy Christmas!" after her then blush like the total idiot I am. I see David looking at me, his eyes wide.

"Was that…?"

"Catriona Thompson," I say, like it's the most normal thing in the world.

"Wow! You could have introduced us."

"I could have…" I say, my brain still trying to catch up with what she was saying, about getting in touch. Probably she was just saying it, for something to say. But still…

"Was she as lovely as she seemed on the Graham Norton show?"

"She was nice," I say. "Yeah, she was nice actually."

I look for Sam, my lifebuoy, and I'm glad to see he is right behind me. I take hold of his hand.

"Hobnobbing, eh?" he smiles.

"Yeah, you know me. Oh, hang on. Is that me or you?" I can hear a phone going, in the recesses of my bag.

"I think it might be mine… no, I think it might be both of ours," Sam says, puzzled.

We head away from the throng of people, and the warmth of the firepit, and I shiver as I rummage in my bag, realising that Sam is right, both our phones are going.

"It's Mum," I say, retrieving my phone first and handing my bag to Sam. He pulls his phone out but I am already answering, half-breathless with a panic that something is wrong with Holly.

"Mum?"

"Oh, Alice, I'm so sorry to disturb you, I really am—"

"That's OK. Is everything alright? Is it Holly?" My mind leaps ahead of me, to all sorts of disastrous scenarios.

"Holly is fine, she's in bed, fast asleep, sugars absolutely fine," Mum says and I think half impatiently, *well what is it then?* "I'm so sorry to bother you, but it's your dad. He's not well, I think it's this cold I've got, but he's suddenly gone a bit faint and I – I think I need to get him home soon."

"What do you mean, faint?" I ask, trying to catch Sam's eye and wondering who has called him. He looks deep in conversation, and serious.

"Oh, just – you know how he gets sometimes, since Covid. I don't want you worrying, or rushing back, but I just wondered if you'd be able to come home not too late. I did message you, sorry, but maybe the messages didn't get to you."

I can't believe I haven't checked my phone till now. I kick myself. "That is fine, Mum, and Dad can always have our bed, if he needs to lie down."

"I'll tell him but to be honest I think he just wants to go home, love. Get in his own bed. You know what he's like."

"Of course, of course. We'll get a taxi back or something. I'll call Brian, see if he's free."

"Oh, love, I'm sorry, I'd forgotten David was driving. I'll pay your cab fare."

"Don't worry about that." It's funny; earlier I was half hoping for an excuse not to come but now I'm here and things are just about to really get going with the music and dancing, I find that I'm disappointed at the thought of leaving early. Especially after that brief conversation with Catriona. My mind floods with the idea of her asking me to be her agent, although I'd barely know where to begin. It can't be that she wants to talk to me about. But what could it be? Maybe nothing. Perhaps she was just being polite. Anyway, I need to sort out getting home now. And I will have to find Lydia and Si to say goodbye. It looks like Sam is just ending his call.

"Alright, alright. Well, we'll see you tomorrow. Looking forward to it."

He takes the phone from his ear and I look at him.

"Sophie," he says, looking a bit concerned.

My jangling nerves have me leaping to more imagined catastrophes. "Is she OK?"

"Yes, she's – well, kind of. I don't know. It sounds like she and Kate have fallen out. And she wants to spend Christmas with us…"

"She – ?" Well that is fine, of course. Sophie is always welcome to come to us, whenever she wants.

"She'll be with us tomorrow. Was that your mum?"

"Yes, it's – Dad's not feeling great. So she just wanted to know when we were coming back really. She's got that cold and I guess he's getting it now too. I said I'd call Brian."

"Oh, OK." Sam actually looks a bit relieved, and I suppose I don't really mind heading back now. I don't belong in this world, really. My world is at home. With my family. "Why don't I call Brian," he suggests, "and you go and tell Lydia, and the others? I'll follow you in."

"Alright," I say and I head past the firepit – now surrounded by ex-smokers who have been lured back into the habit by a few drinks – and into the warmth and hubbub of the Mowhay. Catriona waves at me from a table and I wave back and smile but I am on a mission now and I push through to our group, explaining what's happening.

"I'll take you back," says David decisively. "I can whip you home and be back here in half an hour. That is, if you want to stay, Martin?" He looks at his husband.

"I do quite fancy a dance," Martin admits. "And a

chat with Josh whatshisname." He grins.

"You're not going already are you, Alice?" A flushed-looking Bea puts her hand on my shoulder. "I've barely seen you."

"Yes, well you have been otherwise engaged most of the evening!" I smile, looking across to the man she's been chatting to.

"I suppose I have! *He's a film producer*," she whispers, raising her eyebrows at me. Then, more loudly, "Well look I'll give you a call, let's have a drink over Christmas, OK?"

"Sure – and there's New Year's Eve too."

"Yes, of course! Great. I'll see you soon, one way or another." She hugs me and wishes me a merry Christmas, and I say my goodbyes to Paul and Shona, and ask them to say bye to Lydia and Si for me because I can't see them anywhere and I'm suddenly very tired and very keen to get out of there.

"Come on my lovely," David says, and he leads me out of the door.

"Sam!" I say, seeing him with his phone pressed to his ear. "Cancel the taxi. David's taking us."

"I haven't managed to get through yet anyway," he says. "Thank you David, you're a star."

"That is me, a Christmas star," our lovely friend says, and he links his arms through ours, guiding us through the night towards his car.

5.

In the morning I'm awake bright and early; no hangover at least, which is good. Had we stayed on at the party there is a good chance I'd have tipped past the point of no return, got drunk and embarrassed myself in front of all of Lydia and Si's famous friends. *They're just people*, I tell myself for the last time and smile. I have a sense of relief that it is behind me now and realise I have been feeling a bit tense about it. Now, the way is clear for the end of the school term, Christmas holidays, and the big day itself. The double celebration of Christmas and Holly's birthday.

I make a cup of coffee and tidy up the lounge, opening the curtains to a dark morning but at the sight of the sky gradually lightening down towards the coast, and an excited Poppy following me everywhere and pawing at me, I know exactly what I have to do.

"Come on then," I whisper to her. "Let's go."

She looks at me, head on one side, trying to work out if she's really heard what I said.

I take a step towards the cupboard where we keep her lead and she's bouncing now, overjoyed, like she's never been on a walk before. I can see she's about to bark and I give her a stern look, which she completely ignores. And that's that.

Meg was never a barker but Poppy just can't hold it in. I wonder if maybe she had to before; perhaps she was ignored and now she's desperate for attention, to make herself heard.

Damn, though. I was hoping I could sneak out of the house without waking anybody. But, though it is still not fully light out there, it's not all that late. It's not the end of the world if they're awake. But it does delay my departure somewhat.

Holly emerges, coming sleepily down the stairs in her nightie.

"Is it bedtime?" she asks.

"You can go back to bed if you want to, sweetie," I say, "or go and snuggle in with Daddy. I'm just taking Poppy out for a walk. She got a bit excited."

"Oh Poppy," Holly says, crouching down and cuddling her. "You are silly."

I hear movement in our bedroom. Creaking floorboards. That'll be Sam getting up.

"Go on," I say to Holly, "go up to Daddy and tell him I'm putting the kettle on and that Poppy and I will be back in an hour or so."

I am very keen to go now, get out of the house and down to the beach, just me and Poppy. Some much-needed quiet time. Not that I don't love family walks but if I was to wait for everyone to get up and ready it would take another hour and I think Poppy might burst.

"OK Mummy." Holly kisses Poppy's head and ambles off, in sleepy amiability. She is not always this pliable, I can tell you that.

"Holly," I whisper.

"Yes?" she turns.

"I love you."

"I love you too."

I smile to myself, putting the kettle on for Sam as promised, then I pull on my hat and gloves, fasten Poppy's lead to her collar, unlock the door, and before anyone else can interrupt us, my dog and I head out of the house into a quiet winter morning.

I love the town at this time of day. I mean, of course I love it at all times of day, but there is something extra special about it when there is barely another soul around save for the gulls, and the streets are so quiet. From where we live it's a walk downhill, allowing glimpses of the sea, quickening my heart rate and my pace. Poppy is keen too, pulling ahead, and I try as ever to keep her with me. She's getting better. I don't think she has had a lot of training before so it's all the more to her credit that she's already such a good dog.

As the sun rises, leaking watery light onto the town, I breathe in deeply, taking lungfuls of the fresh air, smelling the familiar saltiness and feeling the cold on my cheeks. We head along Fore Street, Christmas lights still shining at the end of their night-watch duties.

Down to the harbour and there are a couple of other dog walkers out early. We smile and wave at each other, and I greet a red-faced jogger who passes us, puffing determinedly up the steps near the Island car park. We walk across and down to the smallest of the main beaches, but I see a seal has plopped itself onto the sand, and it's not long before Poppy has noticed it too.

"Come on," I say to her, "leave it." She is pulling, intrigued, towards it, but we keep a very good distance, edging along the top of the sand near the café and up the steps towards the beach huts. My legs are feeling the effort but I love it. And now we are up at the base of the Island. *In for a penny, in for a pound,* I think, and trudge determinedly up the steep slope, ignoring the path, and soon enough we reach the chapel, rewarded by having it all to ourselves.

"Ah, Poppy," I breathe, and look down at her, seeing all this walking is wearing off some of her excess energy. I'd forgotten, with Meg getting older, just how much a younger dog can do, and wants to do. She doesn't get a big walk like this every day but at the weekend it's nice to take the opportunity, and the pay-off is that she is much more chilled out for the rest of the day too.

I look out across the sea, which is relatively still, and watch a line of birds heading low across the waves, towards the estuary. I always dread the onset of autumn and winter, but when they arrive I remember the great things about them; the vast skies in their muted colours and the winter birds coming in. Even after all these years I find novelty in the changing faces of the town, the sea and the wildlife. And though winter lays everything bare I do love the subdued nature of it, and feeling that it's OK to stop, not squeezing every drop out of life as I often do in the summer.

I sit on one of the block stone benches, leaning back against the old walls of the chapel. Poppy lies by my feet, content to rest a while. I scan the view of the town, sunlight glinting off windows, pink sky already turning blue, and I listen to the sea, and the gulls who see no reason that anyone should get a lie-in, Sunday morning or not.

In time, I start to feel the cold of my seat through my jeans and I get up, Poppy immediately leaping to her feet, and it's down to the next beach we go. Here, there are surfers already zipped into their skintight wetsuits, brandishing their boards as they head determinedly into the sea. Whether or not they'll get the waves they want today, I don't know, but I do understand the need to make the most of every chance. I really have very little in the way of surfing experience but even just lying on a board and paddling along, over the waves, is lovely. I know this because Ben's now at the point where he wants to have a go and so we've had a few tentative attempts, Sam teaching him while Holly generally stays on the beach (she really does not like going in the sea outside of the summer months) and I have a short time on a board before getting cold and giving in.

"I'm more of a swimmer," I will say, making Sam laugh. But it's true. Ben's small, lithe body is of course far more nimble than mine and he's able to jump to his feet with an ease I can only dream of.

More often than not, I will have a quick dip and then come back in to shore and to Holly, get changed, and then we'll go and fetch coffee and hot chocolate for us all, the brisk walk warming me up.

Poppy does not accompany us for these outings; adding a dog in training to the scenario would definitely be a step too far. But she loves the beach, and right now Poppy would love nothing better than to be running free, but I'm not sure of her yet. She doesn't necessarily like other dogs. She won't necessarily come back when I call her. I extract the long line from my bag and attach it to her collar, unclipping her shorter lead. This way she does get some freedom, and she loves it, dashing at the waves and barking at them, and the gulls, and the cormorants on the rocks, who stay Zenlike, unflappable.

"Poppy!" I call, and she runs towards me, jumping briefly and getting sandy paw marks on my trousers, and then she is off again.

Poppy, Ben and Holly were all very good, Mum said when we got home last night. I could see immediately that we were right to cut short our evening out though. Dad looked very tired and I am always mindful of his health, still weakened from the effects of Covid. Mum did not look well either, sniffing and blowing her nose.

David, our Christmas angel, came in with us to use the loo and, seeing Mum and Dad looking poorly, insisted on driving them home too.

"You'd better hope Martin's not snogging Josh Craven when you get back," I said. "You'll have been gone well over an hour."

David had laughed. "It's fine. Josh will drop Martin like a hot potato when he sees me anyway."

I went to hug Mum.

"Keep your distance, Alice, you don't want these germs. I feel bad for coming over, to be honest. I hope the kids don't get this. Or you and Sam of course!"

"We'll be fine," I said. "Don't worry. Just go home and get a hot water bottle and get into bed. Have you got any Lemsips?"

"Aldi's own make," Dad said, smiling.

"Great, well get one of them each, get into bed and have a good night's sleep, and I'll call you tomorrow. I can go and get you some shopping in if you need anything."

"We'll be fine Alice," Mum said. "You've got enough going on. And at least we'll get this out of the way for Christmas," she added with her trademark positivity.

Let's hope so, I thought, and pushed back that selfish worry again: *What if we get ill for Christmas?* That would really scupper things.

Poppy and I walk all the way to the end of the beach, and I'm starting to flag. Even though I didn't stay out late and didn't drink much. I'm really not used to partying these days.

As we turn around and start to walk back, I think of the beach parties we used to come to here, Julie and I, and the time after we'd just got back to Cornwall and we bumped into Luke by one of the fires – and saw Sam from a distance before he mysteriously disappeared.

We pass the rocks where I first met Sophie and I remember as I always do that little girl who'd spilled some of her bucket water on me and who was so earnest about the creatures she'd found whilst rockpooling. I wonder what she and Kate have argued about. It's not like them, but I know Sophie's found it a struggle, losing her job and coming home, and working at the retreat Kate and Isaac run. It's not ideal for somebody her age, just when she was beginning to really find her independence. It will be nice to have her with us anyway, and I know Ben and Holly will be so excited to have their big sister with us.

"Alice!" I hear as I head up towards the steps away from the beach. I turn to see Natalie, with Keith on his lead. The two dogs are overjoyed to see each other and before we know it they are chasing each other, which is not an easy thing for them or us. Pushing my sandy hair out of my face, I call Poppy to me, clip on her shorter lead again and unclip the long line, then Natalie and I have to try and untangle everything.

"How was the party?" she asks. She would have loved to go, I know. She is still young enough – and single enough – to find the idea of a good night out really enticing.

"It was good thanks, but we had to leave early, Mum and Dad are ill."

"Oh no!" she says, her eyes bright and cheeks rosy. I see her subtly scan my face for signs that I too might be poorly. All of us want to avoid illness at this time of year.

"I know. Just a cold but these things tend to hit Dad worse."

"At least they'll be better for Christmas," she says.

"Hopefully."

Poppy and Keith are still trying their very best to play with each other and it makes me smile. "Want to bring him round tomorrow for a run in the garden, and we can have a cuppa, before we go to the play? Hopefully Keith will be shattered and won't even notice you've gone!"

"I do feel bad for Mum not coming to see Courtney do her thing but Keith's just too little this year. I would offer to stay home instead but… I don't want to!"

I laugh. "Poor Becky. I'd better get home now though, I've been out ages and I haven't had breakfast yet."

By the time we reach the house, I am shattered but feeling smug that I have already got some good exercise into my day. I do my best to rub the sand off Poppy – despite our long walk back up through the streets, she still has half the beach on her – and bring her through to the kitchen, where she immediately goes to her food cupboard. I oblige, filling her bowl and placing it in front of her, listening for signs of life from my family. All is quiet in the house and I wonder if Sam and Holly have dozed off but no, I can just hear the faint sound of some programme or other and I know they will be snuggled in bed watching something on the iPad. I can imagine Sam might be dozing actually, and I don't blame him. I'd quite like to go up there and join him in fact, but no, the day has started now. And Sophie's coming home later. We'd better make her room ready for her.

My mental to-do list starts to run in my mind, like an old-fashioned roll of till receipt: I imagine it unfurling, tasks coming into view and me ticking them off, all day long, until it's finally time to go to bed. It's Sunday though, and I can take my time, and there's no work to get in the way today – and Sam's here too so I know that between us we will get it all done, and by the time Sophie's here she'll have a lovely room to settle in for Christmas and, I guess, all the way into the new year.

First things first, though. Breakfast.

6.

On Monday morning I drive Holly and Ben to school just because I want to go straight to Mum and Dad's and check on them before I start work. Poppy is happy to come along for the ride and I know that they'll be glad to see her too. I haven't told my parents I'm doing this because I know they'll say not to; that I should just get on with my work and stay away from the germs. But I'm hoping they'll either be much better – especially as they are meant to be coming to Holly's play later – or that if they're not, I can do something to help, even just getting them milk, bread and a paper from the corner shop.

Ben slips away as soon as he's out of the car and Holly's not far behind him, though she does at least stop to give me a hug, and then she's swallowed up into the heaving playground. My stomach lurches, I suppose a natural maternal instinct at seeing my children disappear, and made a little more pronounced by the low-level fear I have learned to live with thanks to diabetes. I watch from a distance, and I see Holly – yes, it's definitely her; I recognise her bright red coat – go through the doorway. Then I see Mrs Thomas look up and around, and somehow with her magic teacher eagle eyes she spots me, and she waves and gives me a thumbs-up. It puts a smile on my face and a glow in my heart, that she knows, and she gets it, and she's got Holly's back. And mine, for that matter.

I dread the day Holly starts secondary school and have no idea how I will cope with her being in amongst so many kids, with so many different teachers… but I have to stop, tell myself it's not for now, and put it to one side. I cannot do a single thing about that now and besides, it's four years away yet.

I go back to the car and check Poppy's OK. She wags her tail and looks hopefully at me from her crate.

"Not yet girl, you stay put for now." I close the boot, get in the car, and join the queue of vehicles leaving the school vicinity. I feel sorry for the people who live here, but there is nothing to be done. A lot of these parents, grandparents and carers will have places to be – work, for a start – and a short time to get to them. I know parents get a bad rap and I do also despair of those who don't need to clog up the roads by driving their kids to school (oh, that sounds like me), but life is so busy, so full, for many of us, and it's hard finding a way to fit everything in. Even when we do, I think many of us feel like we're only just getting through the list, not doing anything as well as we would like to. So I'm sorry, school neighbours, but it's just the way it is.

Soon I am on the road out of town, the sky and the sea a matching, sullen grey today. Within minutes I am at Mum and Dad's bungalow and I see that, unusually for this time of day, the curtains are still pulled shut. I sometimes tease Mum that it's a point of principle for her that the curtains must be open as soon as she is up.

"Don't want the neighbours thinking you're having a lie-in, eh?"

"Don't make fun of me!" she will say. "It's a habit I inherited from my mum. Keeping up appearances was very important to her."

I haven't told Mum but I do exactly the same these days.

I leave Poppy in situ for the moment and walk up the neat path, bordered by winter pansies, to ring on the doorbell. No answer.

I try the key, pushing it in and turning it gently then edging the door open.

Now what? Do I call out to them? My heart is beating fast and I tell myself not to be silly; they will be fine. It seems very unlikely that something terrible has happened to both of them.

"Hello?" I say quietly, and listen for signs of life: the radio, for instance, but all is quiet.

"Mum? Dad?" I say their names a little more loudly. Still nothing. So I walk towards their bedroom and listen at their door.

"Oh my god!"

The door flies open and I nearly fall into my mum.

"Alice!"

"Mum!"

"What are you doing creeping about?"

"I just came to see how you are," I say, shamefaced.

"Ah love, we were just having a bit of a sleep in. Your dad had another bad night and I didn't sleep well, but I think the cold's clearing up."

The red skin under her nose and her watery eyes tell a different story.

"Well that's good," I say cheerily, looking into the gloom of the bedroom where I can just make out Dad's shape in bed.

"He's still sleeping," says Mum quietly, and she ushers me away, closing the door behind her.

"I don't want to disturb you, sorry. I just – I wanted to make sure you didn't need anything, before I start work."

"That's very kind of you, love. Would you like a cup of tea?"

"I'll make it," I say, "but I've got Poppy in the car. Do you mind if I bring her in?"

"Of course not. She can go and have a run in the garden if she likes."

"I don't think there is any doubt about that!"

Poppy loves the way Mum and Dad's garden wraps itself around the whole house, even more so when Ben and Holly are here to chase her round and round it. She playfully gambols along in the certain knowledge she could up the tempo and be away from them in a flash. Sometimes, though, one of them will double back and Poppy will be stuck between them both, at which point she'll make a dash past one of them – usually Holly, she knows Ben's faster – and then the chase is really on.

I open the car and Poppy knows immediately where she is. She's on her feet already, tail wagging her whole body. "Come on then!" I glance to the gate to make sure it's secured and then open her crate and she's out, zoomying around the garden like there's no tomorrow.

"I'll be out soon," I assure her then I go back inside to find Mum slumped at the breakfast bar.

"Are you sure you're feeling better?" I ask her.

"Oh yes love, thank you. Just shattered. You know how it is. It takes longer to recover when you're trying to nurse somebody else."

"Well I'll make you a cuppa, give Poppy a run, then I'll get out of your hair. And don't worry about coming to the school play if you don't feel up to it."

"I wouldn't miss it for the world, Alice. Honestly, I always feel worse when I wake up, and in the evening. I should be fine this afternoon. Hopefully after your dad's had a good sleep he'll be up to it too."

As long as you're not coughing and sneezing over everyone, I think, imagining how popular we will be if we manage to pass on this bug to the whole school just in time for the holidays. But it's par for the course, at this time of year, and I am sure Mum and Dad won't be the only ones.

Dad is still sleeping by the time I leave with a panting, happy Poppy, who doesn't especially want to get in the car but does as she's told.

"You're seeing Keith later," I tell her, and her ears prick up at her son's name.

"Thanks for stopping by, Alice," Mum says, still in her dressing gown but looking a lot more human. I made her some porridge, though she protested. Topping it with cinnamon and honey and leaving some in the pan for Dad when he wakes. "It's nice to know you're looking out for us."

"Well you're always doing that for us," I say, hugging her. "See you this afternoon! Tell Dad not to worry about coming though, if he's not well."

"I'll see how he's getting on but I know he won't want

to miss Holly's play. He used to love coming to your nativities; one of the best things about having children, he'd say!"

I get home to find Sophie in the kitchen, only just eating her breakfast. She was tired when she got to us and has been getting up early to do the cleaning at the retreat so she's enjoyed a sleep-in, somehow ignoring her brother's and sister's noisy attempts to wake her.

We let them stay up late to see her, knowing there was no way that they'd be going to sleep anyway, and besides, it's the last day of school today. It's kind of annoying they've made everyone go in for just a Monday but at the same time, we are so close to Christmas now, and school is keeping the children occupied when if they were at home they'd be bouncing off the walls with pent-up excitement and anticipation. Breaking up so late on, we get a few days after new year before they have to start back, which I hope will be nice and chilled.

Poppy runs up to sniff Sophie. She doesn't really know her very well yet so she's keen to check her out. Sophie stoops to ruffle her ears, which gains her instant approval.

"Hello!" I say. "It's so nice having you here." I don't want to ask Sophie about her falling-out with Kate. If she wants to talk to me about it, she will. Or possibly she will talk to Sam. He'll want to know what's going on.

"It's good to be here," she says, smiling over the rim

of a cup of black coffee. "I should have just stuck to the alternate Christmases in the first place."

"But you don't have to! You're not a child anymore. You need to be where you need to be."

"Thank you, Alice. I don't really know where I need to be, but I do know it's not at Mum's place. Not at the moment."

Still, I don't push it. I leave a little gap to see if Sophie wants to expand on this, but she chooses not to, and then her phone pings with a message.

"Great!" she says.

"Good news?"

"Just Amber. She's free today. So I'm going down to hers. If you don't mind?"

"I don't mind at all. I'm working today anyway and then it's Holly's play. Sorry we didn't know you were coming, I could have got you a ticket."

Sophie looks at me, sees I'm teasing her, and grins. "I would go, if I had a ticket," she insists.

"Of course, but I don't think you have to put yourself through that. Holly will just be delighted to tell you all about it later."

"If I'm back," she says. "From Amber's."

"Of course, Sophie. Look, there is no pressure to be here. You know that. I mean, I'm assuming you will be with us on Christmas Day but apart from that, you're young, and you should be out enjoying yourself." I hope I am not saying anything Sam wouldn't agree with. I don't think I am. He's pretty realistic about what life is like when you're in your twenties – although having said that he curtailed his own freedom when he got together with Kate. Quickly, and unexpectedly, he became a dad too. Maybe that makes him even more keen for Sophie to enjoy her freedom now. And especially when the alternative would be settling down with Harry.

I make myself a coffee and leave Sophie to it. She is sleeping in the office/playroom so I'm working in our room. It's not ideal but it's not like it's forever and things are really on the wind-down for Christmas now. Anyway, t's more important Sophie has her own space when she's with us.

In time I hear her come upstairs, and the shower going on in the main bathroom. Twenty minutes later, she pops her head round the door, hair still damp, and I have a momentary flashback to the days when Julie and I lived in David's flat together. "I'm off out now."

"OK, well have a great time, and say hi to Amber. Tell her she's welcome here any time."

"Will do."

And, aside from Poppy, who's settled herself on the bed, next to my outstretched legs, I finally have the house to myself, and even though I am working I am determined to make the most of it because after three-twenty today, this house will be full of noise and excitement, and I won't be able to hear myself think again until next year.

The rest of the morning passes incredibly quickly and I have a long call with Shona, which means by lunchtime I've only just got through all my emails; replying, filing, deleting, blocking spam, of which there is more and more these days. I probably shouldn't have invited Natalie round as I still have loads to do but I'll just have to work this evening, when the kids are in bed.

I heat up some soup and toast a pitta bread, Poppy shadowing me at all times, and I take my lunch to the dining table. I try and do this when I can – actually stop for lunch – but more often than not I can be found eating at my desk. There is no point beginning something else now though as Natalie's due here in about forty minutes.

Punctual as ever, she rings the doorbell at one o'clock, a wriggling Keith in her arms.

"Do you want to take him straight to the garden?" I ask. "I've left the gate unlocked. Poppy's in the kitchen, I'll go and put the kettle on and let her out."

It's still grey, with long, low clouds hanging over us, but it's not as cold as it has been and it's nice to be outside. A robin sings to us from the top of a fencepost while the dogs maraud around the place, using our legs to hide behind, taking it in turns to chase each other.

"Shall we go in and make some coffee?" I suggest. "These two seem pretty well occupied with each other."

"Sounds great." Natalie follows me inside. "I can't believe all that's happened this last year," she says as I put a couple of scoops of coffee into the cafetière.

"I know." I stop what I'm doing and look at her. Twelve months ago, she was still with Rob, still being bullied and controlled by him. And, I'm ashamed to say, I was still irritated by her, and trying to avoid her when I could. I would never tell Natalie that, of course.

"Now look at you!" I say. "It does go to show how life can surprise you. I know things don't always work out for the best but I think this time it's safe to say they have. And how lovely, having your mum with you."

"It is," she says. "And we're used to living together, you know from when Bobby was little, before I got together with that… that dickhead."

"That is being too generous to him," I say, going back to preparing the coffee then sneaking a look outside at the dogs. They are both currently rolling around on their backs, like the pair of wallies they are.

I gently heat some milk while Natalie continues: "I will never, ever forget how kind you and Sam were. You made our Christmas last year, you know. Honestly. I don't know what I'd have done without you."

I put my hand on her arm, seeing she's become a bit teary. She's become a really important friend to me but, a bit like with Lydia, I do sometimes feel a bit older – almost maternal, but I guess more like a big sister – and that's how it is now. I see her self-doubt and her emotions overcoming her, and I put my arms round her.

"We loved last Christmas," I say, "and how would I have managed with Nigel being there, without you and your mum?"

"Nigel!" Natalie looks at me with shining eyes and now a smile on her face. "I'd nearly forgotten about him. How is he? Do you know?"

"Mum and Dad have kept in touch and they say he's a bit cagey about things – you know, healthwise – but he's still getting about in that van of his so I guess he's doing OK. And he met a lady in the summer, in Scotland."

"Ah that's so sweet!" she says, and I realise to her Nigel must seem really quite old but to me he's my parents' age and I'm not ready to think of them as being 'sweet' yet – if ever. I suspect Mum in particular would not appreciate being described in such a way.

"It is pretty lovely," I say. I plunge the coffee and hand a mug to Natalie, then pick up mine. "Shall we go and keep an eye on the crazy dogs? And then–" I check the clock – "we'd probably better think about going. Mrs Thomas is lovely but she's a stickler for punctuality."

"Won't Karen have bagsied you front-row seats?" Natalie asks with a grin, knowing all too well what my mother-in-law is like.

"I've told her it starts fifteen minutes later than it does," I admit, "so with a bit of luck she'll have to join the queue like everybody else."

"That's awful!" Natalie says but we both cackle as we carry our coffees outside.

My plan has worked, I'm happy to say, and Natalie and I arrive at school to find a disgruntled-looking Karen standing with Ron about four-deep in the line of assorted parents, grandparents, brothers and sisters.

Ron smiles at me and I could swear he knows what I've done.

"Hi!" I say sweetly.

"Come and join us," Karen urges, moving back a little as though I should step into the queue with her.

"I don't think we should push in," I say. "We'll go to the back and see you in there."

"She doesn't look overly happy," Natalie observes.

"No. Oops! Ah well, she'll get over it as soon as she sees Holly in her shepherd outfit. It's pretty cute if I do say so myself."

We file along and are soon in the hall, and true to form Karen has saved seats for us, though they're in the second row and it appears that she has been foiled by a rival – a grandma of one of the boys in Courtney's class – who has put coats on two seats either side of her and her husband.

"I'll keep these ones for your mum and dad, Alice," Karen gestures to the chairs on the other side of her.

"No, don't worry, honestly, they'll get sorted when they get here," I say, feeling slightly embarrassed in front of my fellow parents. "Sam will too."

"Well, I don't see why we can't all sit together," Karen huffs but she doesn't push it.

The hall is soon full, and there is standing room only. I twist in my seat and I see Sam at the back, next to Toby's dad. Sam sees me and gives a little wave. The lights go down and I turn to my right, watching Courtney's class then Holly's file in. The music starts and I sit back in my seat, preparing myself for another retelling of the story of Jesus's birth and, no doubt, at some point I will find myself in quiet tears.

Courtney and a little boy in her class have a duet to sing, about how hard it is being inn-keepers and trying to make ends meet. It makes everyone laugh and Courtney is beaming then she spots me, and then her mum next to me, and starts to wave before remembering she's not meant to. "Oh!" she exclaims, and puts her hand to her mouth.

And then baby Jesus is born and Holly shuffles on, apparently forgetting her lines which we have only practised about half a million times and having to be prompted from Mrs Thomas, offstage.

Whatever Holly had done, nothing would stop my predicted tears and Karen, not as lacking in empathy as she might seem, gives my arm a squeeze and sends a smile my way. She may be a slightly pushy grandmother but she would do anything for my children and I can't really complain about that.

Soon enough, the play is over for another year and it hits me that it's the last nativity either of my children will do. That is enough to have me sniffling again.

"Here," Natalie hands me a tissue. "Pull yourself together for god's sake!" But she's smiling and I think it's almost like having Julie by my side. But not quite.

We sit as the lights go up, amidst the hubbub of voices, and I turn again to see Sam. He grins at me then mimes crying. I fake-glare at him.

"Mum and Dad?" I mouth.

He shrugs. We both scour the room. There is no sign of either of them.

7.

As I file out of the hall like one of the school children, I turn on my phone to check for messages but there's nothing from my parents. Maybe Mum fell asleep again. She certainly looked tired. But Dad couldn't still be sleeping… could he?

"I'm going to phone Mum," I tell Sam as soon as I get to him. "Can you wait here for Holly?"

"Of course," he says.

I hadn't told him about going round to see them this morning so he doesn't seem unduly concerned, but I suddenly feel like somebody has dropped a cold stone into the pit of my stomach.

Mum's phone goes straight to voicemail, Dad's too. I know I am panicking, and it doesn't help that my mind is filling with memories of the time Mum became ill, and Paul drove me all the way up to our old home so I could see her in the hospital. I'd been so scared then, and Dad was too. And then years later, we had Holly's admission to hospital. And Bea's husband, Bob, dying, and Luke's parents… Bad things happen, and it's been a long time since I have thought they won't happen to me, or to somebody I love. It's more like why shouldn't they happen to us any more than to anyone else?

When I let the fear in I realise I'm scared something

is just waiting for me now, just round the corner.

But this is not a very festive line of thought and I'm jumping ahead. Jumping to conclusions. And now I have my daughter jumping into my arms, and it takes everything I have to shake those depressing thoughts out of my mind and instead congratulate Holly on her excellent performance.

"I forgot my lines," she whispers to me.

"Did you?" I feign surprise.

"Yes, Mrs Thomas told me the words."

"Well," I say, "you must have covered it up very well because I didn't notice at all, and you spoke beautifully."

Holly beams and flings her arms round my neck then reaches out to hug Sam too so that our heads are squeezed uncomfortably together. We both laugh, and he takes her from me, mock-struggling at the weight of her. "Are you sure you're only going to be seven?" he asks.

"Yes, Daddy!" she giggles.

"Not twenty-seven?"

"Julie thought I was twenty-seven!" she says proudly and I think of my friend and wonder how she is doing; what she is doing right now. That baby must be coming soon.

I remember how it felt, being heavily pregnant at Christmastime, empathising with Mary and wondering how on earth she managed to get on a donkey – and how on earth the donkey managed to carry her. The things animals do for us.

Now Karen has caught up with us and it's her turn to congratulate Holly, and then Ron's, and he takes her from Sam, swings her around, and I'm so grateful they are there and making my little girl feel so good about herself.

We walk outside the playground together and wait for Ben. I hear him before I see him – zooming across the playground with Toby and Ethan and a couple of other boys, and then being halted and admonished by Mr Cleethorpe, the only male teacher at the school, who has been charged with managing the year sixes.

Ben and his friends look slightly shame-faced and apologetic and they continue their journey at a much more acceptable pace, but I don't miss the looks they cast between themselves after they've left Mr Cleethorpe behind them. It's happening, I think, too fast. He'll be year 6 next year, at the top of the school, and already he and his friends are developing that slightly cocky, cheeky attitude. I just hope it's normal, and I hope that he keeps it in check.

We say goodbye to Karen and Ron at the top of the hill and then walk the rest of the way home a little behind Natalie, Bobby and Courtney.

"I'll catch them up," Ben says, and he runs on – and right out into the road, causing a car to do an emergency stop.

"Ben!" Sam roars, and the face I see turning towards us is that of a scared little boy. Shaking, he returns to us, and he flings himself against me, close to tears.

"Sorry," Sam calls to the car driver, who looks a little bit shaky himself, and understandably so. "What were you thinking, Ben?"

I have rarely heard Sam sound so angry. Ben, sobbing now, can't speak. Holly stands next to us, wide-eyed and silent.

"It's OK," I say, I'm not sure to whom.

"It's not OK!" Sam exclaims. "Ben, you could have been killed."

"Just wait a moment," I say to him. "Let Ben calm down." I put my hands on Ben's shoulders, hold him a little way away from me and look at him, trying very hard not to let emotion get the better of me. "You know, Ben, don't you? You know you shouldn't just run into the road like that."

"I-I-I feel sick," says Ben.

"Let's just get home," I say, putting my hand on Sam's arm. I know, of course, that his anger is a symptom of his abject fear at what could have happened. But Ben doesn't know that. "You take Holly, and let's just get home."

And as we walk, our nerves soften a little, and Sam calms, though I can see he's holding Holly so close to him, so fervently. Like me, he can see how things can go wrong, and so very quickly if you're not careful. But we get back to the house in one piece and Poppy comes to greet us, and Ben goes straight into the lounge with her, pushing his face into her soft fur as they fall onto the settee together. Our sweet dog nudges at his face, licking his tears, and it does at least elicit a giggle.

"I'm sorry, Ben," Sam says, sitting on the other side of him. Putting his arm around his son. "I shouldn't have shouted. I was just scared. I'd just – I'd hate anything to happen to you. I shouldn't have been so angry. I just love you so much. It scared me."

"It's OK Daddy," Holly climbs onto his lap, not ready to concede this golden opportunity to be the Good Child, now that we are all safe at home and there are no cars to run us over.

"I'll put the kettle on," I say, feeling like my mum and, funnily enough, just as the water is bubbling, my phone goes and I see it's her. I feel relief flood through me. Firstly that she's phoning, and also because I want to tell her about what just happened and hear her reassurance that it's all OK.

"Hi Mum, how are you?"

"Alice," she says, bypassing the niceties, and her voice sounds strange, and I flood with fear once again. And this time it seems it's justified because Mum, sounding distant and worried, continues, "I'm so sorry to bother you but it's your dad. He's really not very well. I don't know what to do."

8.

I get to Mum and Dad's as quickly as I can, to find the front door is unlocked. I push it open; shout a greeting.

"We're in the bedroom, Alice," Mum calls through and her voice sounds like I've never heard it before. I hurry in, closing the door behind me and scurry along to my parents' lovely, spacious bedroom, which today feels stuffy and has a strange, indefinable odour.

Mum is sitting on her side of the bed and Dad is lying on his, the covers pushed right away from him.

"Mum, Dad, what's happening?"

"I'm so sorry to worry you Alice but I didn't know what else to do. We got as far as the edge of town, to come to the school, but your dad wasn't right."

"In what way?" I ask, trying to make some sense of what is going on.

"I don't – he was, seemed, a little bit out of it. I don't know if it's the cold medicine he's on, or – or something else. But he won't go to A&E."

"Not A&E," Dad groans, and I could swear there's the tiniest smile on his lips, which gives me a little bit of hope.

"But – what then? Is it – is it just a cold, the flu… Covid? What do you think?" These are pointless questions. I already know they don't know.

"It could be any of them. It probably is. I mean, I've felt pretty awful these last few days. Maybe it's just knocked your dad sideways. I'm so sorry we missed Holly's play, and I'm especially sorry to have called you but I just, he seems so poorly."

I look at my mum and I think for the first time ever that, to me at least, she looks old. And there is doubt written right across her face.

This is not my mum, I think. *My mum always knows what to do.* Of course, now I'm a mum myself I realise that can't be true. All along, she has probably been grasping for solutions to things in the same way that I do. It's just she has always managed to carry it off with such aplomb.

"It's OK, Mum. So–" I try to think fast, wonder what might be best – "have you checked Dad's temperature?"

"We don't have a thermometer," she says. "But he does feel warm."

Of course. For some reason we adults treat thermometers as though they are things just for kids.

"Well maybe we'll start there," I say. "I'll pop out to the supermarket and get one. And what about something to eat?"

"He's not hungry, he's barely eaten since Saturday, when we were at your house. Just a bit of toast."

"For you, if not for Dad. But it would be good if he could eat something." I think fast. I want to act. For once, my parents are in need of my help, not the other way around. I must admit that even with the gravity of the situation, it does feel kind of good to be able to do something for them. And I might even be enjoying bossing them about a bit. "Don't worry Mum, I'll be really quick, I'll just pick up a few bits. Dad –" I turn to him – "have you been drinking plenty of fluids? I think you need to. Mum, do you want to get him a glass of squash and see if he can have some of that?"

'Drink plenty of fluids' – I am repeating Mum's usual advice right back to her. Maybe she got it from her mum. Anyway, she doesn't complain now. I don't think she has really noticed, she just nods and goes into the kitchen, returning with a jug of squash and one of the plastic IKEA cups she uses for the children.

I leave the house and get in the car. It's only a few minutes' walk to the supermarket but I feel like I should save any time possible right now. I dash around the shop, finding a thermometer, some paracetamol, some bread, orange juice… ready meals for Mum, some Mini Cheddars and satsumas, and some jelly babies, with Dad in mind. If he's not eating his blood sugar levels might be dipping and with them his energy – well, clearly his energy is dipping. I pick up some throat sweets too and a jar of honey, as well as some honey and lemon teabags. What else? I think, and then think again – *Just get back to them, Alice. This rescue mission isn't your chance to shine. Just go and check on your dad.*

So I do as I'm told (by myself), and I use the self-checkout, thankfully managing the whole thing without having to buzz for assistance once, and then I'm out of there, in the car and heading back to Mum and Dad's.

When I get back in, I'm relieved to see Dad is sitting, propped up by lots of pillows.

"How are you feeling?" I ask but it's a pretty stupid question. His face is flushed and his eyes look very droopy.

"On top of the world, Alice." He manages to smile at me.

"I thought so. Never seen you look so good." I go back to the shopping bag I left in the hallway and rummage around for the thermometer, which I bring back through to the bedroom. Mum is sitting in the chair in the corner now, watching the proceedings.

"Should I do that, Alice?" she asks.

"No it's OK, I'm on it." I bought the same type we have at our house so I know what I'm doing and I just want to check Dad's temperature, and quick. It's pretty high – 38.4.

"Mum, can you just check the NHS website to see when to worry about a high temperature in adults?" I ask. I don't think this would be considered dangerously high but I want to be sure.

"OK," Mum says, fiddling with her phone.

"Have you been drinking, Dad?"

"No! I've been in bed ill since yesterday," he says, outraged.

"Not alcohol," I clarify. "Have you been drinking plenty of the squash Mum brought you – any of it at all, in fact?"

"Bits here and there," he says. I look from the nearly full cup on his bedside table to Mum. She shakes her head.

"You need to drink, Dad," I say. "And what about paracetamol? Have you had some, or ibuprofen?"

"He's been having this," Mum says, picking a bottle

of medicine up off the dressing table. I look at the label and it says it contains paracetamol and also that it can make people feel a bit drowsy so that might explain why Dad is not quite himself. Maybe it's not as bad as it seems.

"He wasn't driving when you went out earlier?" I ask.

"Of course not, Alice," she snaps, and I see the Mum I know again.

"Sorry, that was a stupid question," I acknowledge. "So what do you think you want to do?"

"I don't know." It feels like Mum wants me to tell her what to do. But I don't know either.

"Well it seems like he might just have a fluey thing, but I can't be sure. I suppose, if Dad's alright-ish in himself – *and drinks plenty of fluids –*" I look at him sternly – "then maybe you could hang on till the morning and call your GP then? Or if you feel worse overnight you can call 111. They'd be able to advise you."

It feels like a cop-out, like I'm giving them the brush-off. But I don't really know what else to suggest. I don't think A&E would be the right place to go even if Dad wanted to, and they will, well, probably not laugh us out of there but not be happy to have us taking up their space, their time, and filling the air with germs, passing it on to other patients and staff. Besides, Dad will probably be better off staying home in his own bed instead of having to travel through a cold evening and end up spending maybe hours in an uncomfortable waiting room chair; to me it seems like that could well make him worse. I do think on balance staying put and monitoring how Dad is would be better.

I go into the kitchen to unpack the shopping bag. Mum follows me.

"Thank you Alice," she says. "I think we both feel much better now we've seen you. I just panicked a bit earlier."

"It's understandable, Mum. But if Dad gets worse – or that temperature goes higher, make sure you call 111. I don't mean you can't call me as well! But they can point you in the right direction. Hopefully it will go the other way though, and you might both get a better night's sleep too."

"I do hope so, love. Now look, we've taken enough of your time and those little babies of yours will be wanting their mum before bed." She knows enough not to refer to Ben and Holly as babies in front of them but I know that to her they will always be babies.

"Shall I get you some tea before I go?" I ask. "You must be exhausted."

"No, no, you got me those ready meals. I'll put one in the oven, and see if I can get your dad to eat a bit of it too. But really love, I feel so much better now, and I quite fancy a little drop of wine with my tea."

"I don't suppose a little glass would hurt, Mum, and it might help you sleep better too. Fingers crossed you get a good night."

"Fingers crossed," she agrees.

I say bye to Dad from the bedroom doorway, although I think if I am trying to avoid catching any germs, that ship has sailed by now.

Mum walks me to the front door and hugs me. "We are so lucky to have you," she says.

"And I'm so lucky to have you." I kiss her. "Now go

on, get something to eat and have that glass of wine.
Put your feet up and put something on TV."

"The remote control's all mine tonight!" she says,
trying out a grin.

"Exactly! Make the most of it."

It's already cold outside and the car windscreen needs
to be cleared so I put the blowers on then call Sam while
I wait till I am able to see where I'm going.

"Everything OK?" he asks, concern in his voice.
"How's Phil?"

"I think he's OK. I mean, not OK. He's not well and
he's got a high temperature, but he was sitting up by
the time I left and I think it might be flu… I don't know.
But it's not as bad as I thought."

"That's good news," Sam says. "Are you having tea
there?"

"No, I'm heading home now."

"That's even better news," Sam says. "I'll open a
bottle of wine, shall I? Seems like you might appreciate
a glass tonight."

"And we have to toast our daughter's acting career."
I smile down the phone, long-held memories of my
World of Stationery sales training creeping into my
consciousness.

"Yes, I can hear you smiling," Sam says. He really
does know me too well.

As I approach the edge of town, I'm treated to a view
of the harbour in all its Christmas finery. I must get
down there one evening for a walk. Maybe we'll all go,
on Christmas night, perhaps have a drink at the

Mainbrace too. I sigh and roll my shoulders back, thinking everything is OK, and now we have Christmas to look forward to. Some time off together, and some family time, with Sophie as well. As long as Mum and Dad are better for the big day, and none of us catch their lurgy, all is set for a lovely Christmas and it's time now to let myself relax into it.

9.

One slight problem with having Sophie at home again is that when she is late out – as she was last night – Sam and I are both unable to fall asleep till we know she is safely home. But we don't want to let her know that; she is quite able and welcome to go out and come back when she wants to, but it doesn't stop us worrying for her safety. Sam in particular.

When we hear the door go and a single bark from Poppy, followed by some soothing words from Sophie, I think we both breathe a sigh of relief, and it seems like just seconds before Sam's breathing slows and deepens. I hear Sophie's soft tread on the stairs, then she uses the bathroom and heads back down again to her room.

Soon, all is quiet in the house, save for the familiar buzzing sound from my radio alarm clock, and the occasional creak as the pipework settles for the night.

I will my mind to switch off, and wish that I found it as easy as Sam seems to, but now my mind is fizzing with thoughts and I check my phone to make sure Holly's blood sugars are alright, then a niggle about Dad takes hold and I worry that maybe we should have got him to A&E, or got a doctor out to him, if house visits are a thing these days. I am touched but also a bit scared by how Mum seemed to look to me for an

85

answer. I am well used to responsibility these days but do I want to be responsible for my parents too? I mean, I would do anything for them, of course, but thinking that the tables might be slowly beginning to turn in our relationship is like looking down from a dizzying height, into a great abyss. Because once your parents become reliant on you, and not the other way around, your whole understanding of the way life works must change. And, as with being a parent, you must just have to grab the bull by the horns and make decisions when you don't really know they're the right ones.

Anyway, I am letting my mind run away with me. We are not at such a point right now, and Mum is just tired and run-down after being ill herself. She will be back to her usual self soon. And what use will it be lying awake worrying about it anyway? I plump my pillow, gently so as not to wake Sam, lie on my back, and imagine being in one of Lizzie's yoga classes… I try some breathing exercises, which help to calm me, and then I try a technique where I tense and relax each part of my body in turn then begin counting down from 1000 (yes, really). I visualise the numbers, which appear in bubble-writing form in my mind, and try not to get annoyed that I am still counting at 792. But I don't remember much after that.

In the morning, I wake to a bed and a room to myself, the door closed and the sounds of family life drifting up from downstairs. I hear Holly's voice, then Sophie's, then Sam's. I hear Ben giggling manically, saying Poppy's name, and assume that either he is chasing her round the downstairs rooms or that she's trying her best to lick his face off, as she likes to do to him specifically. I smile and stretch. I am not officially off work but, talking to Shona yesterday, we've both agreed to just keep an eye on emails when we can. Shona has her sights set on Josh Craven as a new client, and I know she'll be doing some digging there, but that is not for me to worry about.

I sit up and drink the glass of water I left on my bedside table last night, then I check my phone. A message from Sam:

Let me know when you're awake and I'll bring you a coffee x

Could I love this man any more?

I'm awake! xx

I check Holly's app even though Sam will have everything covered. But it's hard to explain what a sense of reassurance it can bring, to see that she is doing OK.

I message Mum and Dad on our family group:

Morning. How are you both today? X

Then I go through to the bathroom and when I get back there is a message from Dad:

Morning, daughter. We are both feeling much better. Thanks for looking after us both. Love Dad xx

So it appears all is well with the world. And it only gets better when Sam opens the door, bearing not just a coffee but a plate with a warm Danish pastry.

"Well this is a very nice," I say, snuggling back under the covers, all my fears and worries from the middle of the night having vanished with the darkness.

"Soph went out to the bakery," he says, "and you were so fast asleep when I got up I didn't want to wake you."

"Happy Christmas," I say happily.

"We're not there yet," he says.

"But we are. It's the Christmas holidays, Sophie is here. We're together. Christmas has begun."

He puts the cup and plate on his bedside table and slides onto the bed next to me. "Just for a moment."

I wrap my arms around him, pull his head gently onto my chest and press my face into his curly hair. There are a few wiry greys making themselves known these days, but they blend in well and you'd have to be pretty close up to notice them.

I kiss him and hear him mumble something into the duvet. "What was that?"

"Happy Christmas, Alice."

The five of us, and Poppy, go for a late-morning walk along the beach and, at Sam's insistence, I have brought my swimming things. Sophie has hers too. We go to the smallest beach, where it's sheltered, and I'm pleased to see that it's seal-free today as well.

"Are we really doing this?" Sophie asks as we strip off and walk gingerly down to the shore.

"Yes!" I laugh. "You'll love it."

"I'm pretty sure cold-water swimming's for middle-aged women," she grins at me. I splash her and she shrieks. Then I dash in through the gentle waves, trying to imagine that it's a hot summer day. When I'm waist-deep I look round and see Sophie still picking her way through the shallows. "Come on!"

"I might just get out again," she says. "Sorry Alice."

"Your loss!" I call, and I push on alone into the deeper water, not wanting to go too far but wanting to be able to swim. And, as is always the case, once I'm in and I've submerged my shoulders, it's lovely. I won't stay in long but I will make the most of these peaceful moments; it's just me and the water and the birds on the rocks. I swim parallel to shore one way then the other, and then I float on my back for a while, my head resting on my tow float as I would like to keep my hair dry if possible. It is tucked into a woolly hat in a vain attempt to keep a little bit of the heat in, and to hopefully save me from having to walk home with cold, wet locks.

Gazing up at the sky, I can't help but smile, and then I laugh, thinking of what Sophie said. Maybe this is for middle-aged women, but I don't take that as an insult. I am stronger at this age than I once was, and more sure of myself, and I don't worry so much what people think of me. I do miss the energy I had in my younger years, that's true, but I like being this age. Despite the weight of responsibility it seems to bring with it, and worries about children – and parents – in many ways I feel happier now than I've ever been.

I watch a small family of gulls pass overhead, and I right myself, taking a few slow breaths as I swim back to the shore.

"Mummy!" Holly shouts, running towards me then shrinking away again as she remembers I am soaking wet.

"Good?" Sam asks, wrapping a towel around me and kissing me.

"Very."

"I might join you one of these days."

"You'd be welcome to," I say, and he would of course, but I do relish those moments away from everything. The absolute peace it brings. Anyway, I know he won't – or not till the summer at least. He can just about bear being in the sea in his wetsuit with Ben and the board but I don't think Sam will be winter-swimming just for the sake of it.

I get changed in the public toilets, which have a sticker pronouncing them winners of a competition back in 2003. I like the fact we're still proud of that.

In the summer, these toilets are always busy, the floor soaked and covered with sand and soggy toilet roll. In the winter they are closed for part of the time but as town begins to get busy again, building up to New Year's Eve, they are open once more but right now they are barely used and so the floor, though cold on my bare feet, is clean. I struggle into my clothes, my skin still ever so slightly damp, and push all my wet things into a bag. When I emerge, my family are waiting for me.

"These guys want a hot chocolate," says Sam.

"Sounds good to me!" I take Holly's hand and we walk along the back streets towards the harbour, where we sit at an outside table and order five hot chocolates with the works. I know I'll find it too much but I would feel like a killjoy if I just had a coffee.

Holly yawns.

"Feeling sleepy?" I ask her, running my fingers over her forehead and through her fringe. She nods.

"Maybe we should head home soon," I say to Sam.

"Sounds good to me. I need to watch *Elf*."

"Need?"

"Yes, we need to watch it, don't we Ben? Otherwise it won't be Christmas."

"I LOVE *ELF*!" shouts Holly.

"You've never even seen it," says Ben.

"I have."

"When?"

"Who cares?" Sam says, exasperated. "We'll all watch it this afternoon and then we'll know that all of us have definitely seen it. OK?"

"I've still got some presents to buy," Sophie admits. "So I might have to give *Elf* a miss."

"Do you want some company?" I ask, wondering if she's just trying to get out of the film. Of course that's not my motivation at all and this is an entirely selfless offer. "I've got a couple of last-minute things to get too."

"That would be great." She smiles and I think she means it. I don't want to push my company onto her, but it would be nice to spend some time with Sophie and make sure she's OK too. I'm very aware that as an older sibling she has to fit around our family life, and I never want her to feel on the outside. I wish she had her own permanent room at our house but then, as Sam says, she's old enough to have her own place really. Even so, it can't be easy for her, having separated parents, and younger half-siblings, and now she seems to have fallen out with her mum. Hopefully we can help her sort that out while she is staying with us.

It's really nice shopping with Sophie anyway. We go into most of the shops on Fore Street and she gets a couple of books for Ben and Holly, and I help her choose a scarf for Sam. She wanted to buy him a jumper but I told her not to. I know she won't have loads of money at the moment. "Honestly Sophie, he will just be glad you're here. Your presence is a present. Sorry, that was terrible."

"I'm glad I'm here too," she says. "And I'm really shopping with you, Alice. It's nice to be home."

"I'm having a great day!" I say, touched at her words but feeling slightly bad for Kate. I am sure she'd be hurt at the thought Sophie still describes Cornwall as home. "Look, should we stop and have a mulled cider at the Mainbrace? Once we've done our shopping, I mean."

"Yes! That would be brilliant."

I smile, and squeeze Sophie's arm lightly. What a thing to have watched her grow up, seen her through all the difficult times of being a teenager, and coping with moving to Devon, and becoming a big sister three times over. She has been amazing really, and I think we have been lucky that she's such a steady person. And now to be able to have a drink with her, go shopping with her, feels really special.

While she is off looking for something for Amber, I take the chance to pick up a couple of extra little bits for

Sophie. I know full well that Ben and Holly will have way too much again because both Karen and Mum can't help themselves, spotting things throughout the year and then somehow being surprised by how much there is when Christmas comes around. And then we have the fact it's Holly's birthday too. She will be doubly lost in presents. I want to make sure Sophie has plenty too.

I go back to the bookshop and pick up a couple of novels I think she'll like, and I go into the lovely soap shop and get her a gift set with socks, an eye mask and some facial oil. A selection pack of chocolate bars, which is a must, and a few little odds and ends like playing cards and a drinks coaster and some gloves and chocolate coins, so that I can do her a stocking too. I think she will appreciate that.

By the time I meet up with her again, I have a lot more than I'd planned, but all feels right with the world now.

"Get what you wanted?" I ask and she nods. "Come on then, let's go and have that drink."

10.

I couldn't have planned it better if I'd tried. It is low tide and the shanty-singers are gathering on the harbour beach. And, as if that wasn't enough, at exactly the moment Sophie and I arrive at the pub, a family get up and vacate their table. I don't even have to tell Sophie; clearly a seasoned professional, she is quick as a flash, slipping onto one of the benches whilst simultaneously shining a guileless smile at a group of men who look like they've been waiting a while, watching for a seat like the gulls who are keeping a beady eye out for any dropped or unguarded crisps or chips.

I look from Sophie to the men and see they send good-natured smiles her way. It helps that she's an attractive young woman, of course. I don't know if I'd get away with it these days. Julie probably would.

"Do you want some chips as well?" I ask Sophie.

"Yes please! I'm starving! Thank you, Alice. Can I give you some money…" She reaches into her bag.

"Don't even think about it!" I laugh. "How often do I get to buy my stepdaughter a drink and some chips? And Sophie, you've saved me from an afternoon watching *Elf*! I owe you one."

She laughs too.

I see a couple of familiar faces in the pub but for the most part it is heaving with holiday-makers, treating themselves to a Christmas on the Cornish coast. Who can blame them? Away from home and all the inevitable responsibilities that come with it – albeit also without the familiarity of their own kitchens to cook Christmas dinner in – it's no wonder the atmosphere is so joyful.

I order our chips and drinks, carrying the hot ciders carefully through the pub and trying not to spill a drop. Steam rises pleasingly from the mugs as I move into the outdoors and place them triumphantly on the table in front of Sophie, then move to sit next to her. We both now have a view of the harbour and can watch the singers as darkness creeps in across the sea, claiming the town for itself once more. The lights are already lit along the harbour pier and on the boats and if I'm not careful I could find a tear or two in my eyes. I still love this town with all my heart, and every now and then it still takes me by surprise that this is my home now. I belong here. I don't ever want to take that for granted.

My other motivation for sitting beside – rather than across from – Sophie is that I think it's easier to talk this way. Without the face of the person opposite staring at you.

"So," I say. And I do turn to her, and I'm pleased she returns my gesture, her eyes meeting mine.

"So," she says, and I see it doesn't take much to peel away the carefully constructed layers of cheer to reveal the sadness in Sophie right now.

"How's Harry?" I ask, hoping I am not jumping in too deep too soon.

"He's OK," she says. "Thanks."

"That's good. He's a nice…" My sentence dwindles. What do I call him? He is not a boy, but young man makes me sound like I could be his grandma. "Bloke?" I say with a question mark, feeling woefully inadequate. But it makes Sophie laugh.

"He is a nice bloke," she agrees.

"And are things still good with you two?"

"Yeah, they are, I guess. Actually – he's asked me to move in with him."

"Has he?" I ask, trying to work out what my reaction to this should be. First and foremost for Sophie – I cannot tell if she likes the idea or not. Secondly for Sam, and Kate – what would they think about their daughter moving in with somebody at such a young age? Well, I know of course, what Sam thinks – and I see he was spot on, about Harry wanting to settle down already. But, while I wouldn't want to upset him, this is not Sam's decision to make.

"Yeah. But, I don't know."

"OK. You're not sure you want to move in with him?"

"No, I'm not. And I don't know – I don't really know if I want to be with him at all anymore." She sighs and looks close to tears.

"Well that's OK," I tell her. "Sometimes things run their course."

"But he's lovely," she says.

"I know he is. But sometimes that's not enough, unfortunately. You have to really want to be with somebody to move in together. And you need to be compatible. It can be hard work, you know."

"Not for you and Dad."

"Even for me and Sam," I say. "We have had our moments, believe me."

"I do remember that time…" she begins.

"What time?" I ask, genuinely interested to know when she thinks we had difficulties.

"When it was my fault. That Christmas."

"Sophie!" I exclaim, my mind shooting immediately back to the time she means. When Sam was back from Wales and Sophie wasn't happy that we were together – and neither was Kate. "That was a long time ago, and that was absolutely not your fault!"

The barmaid comes out with two bowls of chips, and a little basket of condiments. I smile and thank her then turn back to Sophie. "I had no idea you thought that, or that you remembered it, really."

"I really remember it, and I feel worse and worse about it. You split up because of me."

"We split up because of life," I correct her. "And you can't at this age feel bad for something you did when you were – what? Eleven? You were so young. And you'd just discovered Sam wasn't who you thought he was."

"My biological dad," Sophie says, selecting the right words, which I am grateful for.

"Your biological dad," I confirm. "And that was my fault you found out that way! Well, and Julie's I suppose. But I shouldn't have told her."

"No, Mum should have told me!" Sophie says. "It shouldn't ever have been a secret."

"Well if that's the case, you can say the same about Sam, not just Kate. They are both your parents, and it is down to both of them. But I think it's clear we were all a bit in the wrong, or to put it another way, we were all trying to do what we thought was right, sometimes for you but sometimes for ourselves," I admit. "The only one not in the wrong was you. You were a really young child. And you were stuck in the middle of it all. No wonder you ran away."

"I don't think I meant to run away as such," she says quietly. "I wanted attention. Dad's, especially."

"Well of course. And he'd gone off to Wales to be a student." I find it painful even now to think about that time. "But Sophie, I can say now, and I am sure that Sam would agree, you did absolutely nothing wrong, and you can stop beating yourself up about it, OK?"

"OK."

"Anyway," I try to bring us back round to safer ground, "I didn't even mean back then. I just mean in day-to-day life. You need to be solid to live together, I really think that. When other stresses creep in – work stress, friendship issues, health, whatever – it can impact your home life and you have to really want to be together to get through the hard times."

"Mum thinks I should do it."

"Really? Kate wants you to move in with Harry?" That does surprise me. Or does it? When I think of her when we first met – a single mum, trying to start a business, drinking too much and looking for a partner in crime for nights out but really just looking for a man to settle down with, as if that would solve everything – I can see why Kate might think Sophie should accept Harry's offer. He seems nice and reliable. And now I don't quite know what to say as I don't want to talk over Kate's wishes. But at the same time, I don't want

Sophie to move in with somebody just because her mum wants her to. That can't be right.

"I think she just wants me to move out!" Sophie laughs without mirth.

"I really don't think that would be the case," I say. "Your mum adores you. My god, I remember when it was just you two, and..."

"But it's not anymore, is it? Not just us two, I mean. It's Isaac, and Jacob, and the business. I'm grateful to her for letting me work and live there while I look for another job but God it's been hard. I get it. I'm not a kid anymore. I don't fit into their life."

Tears are threatening now, I can see them. It nearly breaks my heart and I see again that little girl, from so many years ago, missing her dad and understandably struggling to share him with me when he came back to Cornwall for the holidays. It was my decision then to break up with Sam and it was the right one. And now, in the long run, it has worked out anyway. But there was no guarantee that it would have done.

"Sophie," I say, "I'm so sorry you feel like this. And you know, I was thinking earlier that I wish we had a better room for you to stay with us. I don't like you feeling you're being squeezed in, or that Ben and Holly might come first." I don't know if she does feel like that and I don't want to put the idea in her head, but I think right now I need to be open and clear with her. "You will always have a home with us, and I am really sure your mum feels exactly the same, if not more so. She absolutely thinks the world of you and she always has. And she always will."

"Thank you, Alice. I always feel better talking to you."

"I'm glad you know you can, any time, about anything." I want to know if this is what she and Kate have fallen out about – Harry. But I think it might also be good to get some food into her. "Look, the chips are getting cold, so let's get stuck in, but we can stay on for another drink if you like and we can talk some more."

I really want to think about what Sophie's said, and how she feels. I wonder if, seeing her so grown-up and independent, we have missed something; messed up somewhere. And I think about how I feel with my own mum and dad, that I still want to be their daughter. That I am not quite ready to swap places and take on responsibility for them, but I know I might not have any choice one day.

Sophie, twenty years younger than me, needs her mum and dad as much as she ever has. I need to make sure she knows that they know that.

As we pour vinegar and shake salt over our chips, the shanty singers start up their version of the St Day Carol. I smile at the thought of Dad singing it to Holly and I hear those words, sung so beautifully now:

And the first tree in the greenwood, it was the holly.
Holly! Holly!
And the first tree in the greenwood, it was the holly!

A slight breeze blows in from the sea and ruffles the bunting and lights that are strung above the tables, gently shaking the lights on the boats and around the harbour. I move closer to Sophie, putting a chip in my mouth with one hand and putting my other arm around her. I'm glad she leans her head against me and doesn't seem to feel awkward, and we sit like that for some time, enjoying the singing and just being close to each other.

When the set of songs is over, the crowd that has gathered erupts into applause and it lifts me – and I think Sophie too.

"I'll get us another drink," she says, and I'm pleased to see she is smiling now.

As she disappears into the pub, I hear my phone go and I'm jolted guiltily by the thought of Mum and Dad. I had planned to check in with them again. I take my phone from my pocket and see it's actually Julie. Oh my god…

"No I haven't had it yet!" she says the minute I answer the call. "Before you have the chance to ask."

I laugh. "As if I'm even interested. God, I'd pretty much forgotten you're pregnant."

"Well everyone keeps asking – as if I'd have had the baby and forgotten to mention it."

"I remember that well," I say. "But it's just because they care."

"Yeah, yeah. Anyway, it's doing my head in, being pregnant. I've done enough glowing. I just want the baby now. It's two days late already."

"Getting its sense of punctuality from you?" I suggest.

"Hey!" At least she is laughing. "Where are you, anyway?"

"Hang on…" I change the call to video. Turn the camera outwards and move it around so that she can see the harbour.

"Oh Alice, I wish I was there."

"I wish you were too. So much. But you're happy? You're set for Christmas?"

"Well, apart from this baby refusing to show up, yes."

"Maybe it really will be born on Christmas Day as well. Share a birthday with Holly. And Jesus."

"God I hope not," she says then realises what that sounds like. "I don't mean it like that. I just mean, I want it out now. And I want to be home on Christmas Day. At least Mum's here so whatever happens, Zinnia's got company. But I don't want them spending Christmas just the two of them."

"No, that would seem a little bit sad. But what will be will be."

"I know. It's true. Hang on, is that Sophie…?"

I turn to see that it is indeed Sophie, delivering two more mugs of mulled cider.

"Hi Julie!" she says as I hold the phone up so she can see who she is talking to. "Have you had it yet?"

Julie holds her tongue. "I thought you were up in Devon, Soph?"

"Yeah, well, I was going to be but I've… fallen out with Mum." She looks at me as if to ask if it's OK to tell Julie that. I shrug and nod. "Harry wants me to move in with him, and Mum wants me to move in with him… but I don't know."

It's interesting seeing Sophie talk like this to Julie when it was hard work getting the story out of her. I think with Julie she is more keen to impress and pretend she's not as bothered as she really is.

"Well look Soph, you're still young. You know when Alice and I moved back to Cornwall we were older than you, and I'd broken up with somebody I was engaged to. I felt like I was too young even then. And I was nearly thirty."

That probably sounds really old to Sophie. I think, *Hang on, Julie. Don't go giving advice to Sophie, especially when it's not advice Kate would agree with.* But at the same time I do agree with her and, while I don't want to upset Kate, that's preferable to Sophie making a huge mistake, living with a partner she's not sure about. And curtailing her young, free days to please somebody else, whether that's her boyfriend, or her mum, or both of them. And at least this way it's Julie giving the advice, and not me.

"And Alice had a bad time at your age, didn't you Alice?"

If I could have stared daggers at Julie without Sophie noticing, I would have. But Sophie's head springs round to me. "Did you, Alice? With Dad?"

"Yes," I say. "I did have a bad time. But no, not with your dad. Of course not your dad. But it was a long time ago, and it's a long story. I will tell you sometime, but not now."

Thankfully Julie gets the message and, to her credit, looks unusually apologetic. "Alice is right, sorry. It's a long story. Not for now. This is meant to be all about being cheery and peace on Earth, good will to all men and all that jazz."

We chat for a couple more minutes and then Julie has to go, and it's not long until we do too. I think we have taken as much liberty as we can this afternoon. We walk arm in arm up the hill towards home and it feels lovely. I have a slightly fuzzy feeling from the cider and I am looking forward to getting home and settling down for an evening in. No school, no work… I sigh at the thought.

"You'll get things sorted with your mum, you know." I squeeze Sophie's arm with mine.

"I know. I just – I feel bad, but I had to get away for a bit. Even though it's Christmas."

"Especially because it's Christmas?" I suggest.

"You're quite wise, aren't you Alice? For an old bird?" Sophie pushes it a bit and it makes me laugh, then she is giggling and that is how we arrive home, in the best of spirits, and happy to find that Sam, Ben and Holly are too.

"Have you two been drinking?" Sam asks, eyeing our rosy cheeks suspiciously.

"No… well, maybe a little mulled cider… at the Mainbrace."

"We sat outside and the shanty singers were on the harbour, and… I hope you had a nice afternoon, Dad."

Sophie doesn't want Sam to feel like he's missed out and she sits down next to him, rests her head on his shoulder.

'Thank you' Sam mouths at me, but it really was my pleasure. It's been a lovely afternoon and I am so pleased Sophie opened up to me. Hopefully she and Kate can sort it out at New Year. "Your mum rang," he says, "on the landline, about ten minutes ago. I just missed it and I tried to call her back but there was no answer."

Mum, Dad and Karen are the only people who ring our landline these days – them and the wannabe scammers, but even they seem to have given up lately. I take my own phone with me through to the kitchen, so I can make some tea while I chat to Mum. I try her mobile, then their landline just in case, and there is no answer on either. Then, just as I'm pouring boiling water into the teapot, she calls back.

"Alice?" she says, not waiting for me to say hello and then, for the third time in the last four days, Mum says, "I'm so sorry to bother you, but it's your dad." She pauses, maybe swallows. In fact it seems to take her a moment to speak again. "He really isn't well, Alice. He's been taken to hospital and it isn't… it doesn't… it doesn't look very good."

11.

My warm, cidery glow is gone in an instant.

"He's – what? I thought you were both feeling better."

"We were!" she insists. "This morning, we were watching the TV together and your dad was talking about maybe trying a little walk later. You know what he's like. But this afternoon, he started to have some problems breathing, and his temperature had spiked again and I called an ambulance. He didn't want me to but I didn't know what else to do. I didn't want to bother you again—"

"Mum!" I say sharply. "As if you'd be bothering me. Where are you? Are you at the hospital too?"

"Yes, I am. I'm outside at the moment, so I can't stay on long, I need to get back to him. But I had to let you know what was happening. I'll call you later when I know more."

"Mum," I say sternly, pulling myself up to my full height. "I'm on my way."

I take one tiny moment to try and think things through but it's hard with my heart beating ten to the dozen, and my own breath shallow. I call Sam into the kitchen on the pretext of needing a hand and I tell him what Mum told me. I take a couple of scalding gulps of my tea, which sobers me up even more.

"I need to get to the hospital, but I've been drinking," I say, close to tears.

"How many did you have?"

"Only two – mulled ciders – but I don't think I should drive, do you?"

"No, I guess not. And I don't think you should anyway. You're upset. I'll take you."

"What about Ben and Holly?"

"They can stay with Soph."

I know I need to talk to him about Sophie but it isn't the right time. "As long as she doesn't mind."

"She won't," Sam says confidently.

I hope not. I don't want her feeling taken advantage of but I know that she'll understand this is a bit of an emergency. At least I think it is. I know when Mum called the other night it turned out OK, but Dad wouldn't have been taken to hospital unless it was necessary, would he?

It is hard leaving because Holly really doesn't want me to, and I really don't want to tell her that Grandad is poorly, so she doesn't understand why I'm going out again when I've only just got home.

"I'll be back in a bit," I say, really having no idea if this is true. She clings to me, crying. It makes me want to cry too. "Ben, are you OK?" I ask, knowing that just because he doesn't make a fuss doesn't mean he isn't bothered as well. He shrugs. And Sophie, amazing Sophie, comes to my rescue.

"I actually need you two to help me with something," she says.

That gets both their attention.

"What is it?" asks Holly.

"I can't say in front of your mum, OK? We'll have to wait till she goes out. But I think you're going to like it."

"Are you going now, Mummy?" Holly says, her eyes still shining with pools of tears as she pushes me towards the door. It makes us laugh at least.

And I'm glad to have Sam driving me. Not just because I've had a couple of drinks but because I am so on edge, so scared. I want to call Mum back but I also don't want to speak to her until I can see her in person.

"Deep breaths, Alice," Sam says as we head out of town and into the depths of the winter night. Weird how four months ago it would still be light at this time; still warm, and it would feel like there were hours left in the day. Now, I could happily go to bed at this time if I had the chance.

Looking back over my shoulder, I see the town lit up exactly as it was when I left Mum and Dad's house… when? Was that really just last night? It seems like days ago. I can't help the sob that comes unbidden at the thought of Dad being whisked away to hospital: the 'what if' of him not returning home. I know, I know, I have minimal information and no reason to jump ahead like that but I feel like for years now I have been preparing myself for this eventuality. Knowing my parents can't last forever and that the chances are they will die before me. It's all very morbid I suppose but I like to think it is realism too. Still, I don't suppose we can ever really prepare ourselves.

Anyway, *Breathe, Alice* (Lizzie), *Deep breaths* (Sam). I heed their advice. Calm my mind. Know that I know nothing right now. But I am both relieved and terrified when we reach the hospital – desperate to get to Mum and yet fearful and wishing I could just stay in this nice warm car with Sam. He asks if I want him to come with me, but I tell him to get back to the kids.

"Mum and I – and hopefully Dad too – can get a taxi back later."

"You'll do nothing of the sort!" Sam says. "Give me a call when you know what's going on. I'll come and get you."

"You –" I know there is no point protesting, and also that I would do exactly the same for him. "OK. I'll let you know. Thank you, Sam." I hug him tightly. "I love you."

"I love you too." He smiles and strokes my cheek. "Now go and find your mum and dad, and give them my love."

"I will."

I turn and head across to the brightly lit building, turning to wave to Sam, who I know is waiting to see me go in, then with a long, deep breath turning back and walking headlong into the gaping mouth of the waiting hospital.

12.

There is a large Christmas tree inside the doorway, all of its baubles displaying faces and names of staff members with a huge Thank You star at the top. I briefly notice a sign next to it saying patients can sponsor a star to say thank you to somebody who has gone above and beyond for them – the money goes to the hospital's Friends society.

I have nothing against a Friends society of course, and the people who belong to it are kind-hearted, generous volunteers, but should a vital public service need to have a charitable arm? But that is not for now. Now, I need to find my dad, and my mum.

I go to the reception desk, give the details Mum has texted to me, and I am sent down a maze of shiny, clinical-smelling corridors. It feels like I am going against the flow of the other people here, passing by doctors, nurses and other hospital staff who barely glance at me, and patients of varying levels of mobility. A man in a Christmas hat moves tentatively past on crutches, as though he is just getting used to them. The woman with him, wearing a Snoopy Christmas jumper, smiles at me. Another man, about my age, pushes a frail-looking woman along in a wheelchair. A little girl skips along asking her dad, "Can we really go home now?" I smile at them, missing Holly and Ben madly and wishing I was just at home with them. Sinking onto the settee with a cup of tea in my hand and my children either side of me.

I stifle a sob, feeling very alone and wondering if I should have accepted Sam's offer to come in with me. But it will take him a while to drive back home and the kids need him. Somebody needs to be on hand for Holly. It's not fair to leave Sophie with all that responsibility.

I walk on, checking the signs and finding the one to the ward I need. I hurry along the corridor, press the buzzer, give my name and am allowed through. A kind orderly shows me to a single room where my mum sits beside an empty hospital bed.

"Mum?" I gasp, panic gripping me at the sight of her sad figure folded into a chair next to an empty, spotless bed.

"Alice!" she stands, and again I see her in an older form. This woman who has been strong, vibrant, fun and playful now small to my eyes.

"What's happened?" I ask weakly. "Dad?"

"Oh no, love," she gets my meaning immediately. "No, he's been taken for some tests. No, he's, he's not..." She breaks down in tears and I hug her, and we hold each other tightly, for some time.

Mum breaks away first, steps back. Does her best to straighten herself up and wipe away her tears. "Oh love, it's good to have you here."

"What's happening, Mum?" I ask, following her lead, trying to push my emotions back into their box and take a more reasoned, sensible approach. I switch into problem-solving mode, though I don't think there is any problem here that I could possibly solve. I have limited medical knowledge and what I do have relates mostly to Holly, and managing diabetes. It's not going to get me far. "What are they testing Dad for?"

"Let me try and remember what the doctor said. It's so much to take in. I wish we'd got him here though, last night. I should have followed my gut. I knew it. I knew I should."

"But Dad didn't want to come. And yes he was poorly but he was OK too. And you've been ill as well," I tell her. "But what's going on now? What are they testing Dad for?" I ask again.

"He's – he's not breathing well. And I think that bug's gone to his chest. You know how things get him these days. So they say they think he's got a chest infection and they think it might be – it might be… sepsis… as well. But they're scanning his lungs right now," she clarifies. "They want to see what's happening, if there's fluid on them. I can't think what else they said…" I can see she's struggling to get it all straight in her mind.

"Sepsis?" I ask, picking up on the word. It's something I don't think I had even heard of till a few years back but I know that it can be really nasty.

"Alice," Mum says, looking me straight in the eye. "I have to warn you, he's very poorly."

I am immediately a little girl. The thought of my dad, vanquished by illness, struck down and confined in a hospital bed. The man who used to carry me high on his shoulders as he strode along the street. Who would scoop me up if I'd fallen over; place me squarely on the kitchen table and clean my grazed knee, telling me to hold onto his hair and pull it when the wipe made my skin sting.

'Very poorly' feels like code to me. It sounds far too subtle and minimising, like something you'd say to a child.

"What do you mean, *very poorly*?" I ask Mum, in a harsher voice than I mean to.

"He's, you know I said he wasn't himself yesterday, when we were coming to see Holly's play?" I nod. "He's, I think he's hallucinating. It's probably his temperature, or the infection… I don't know. He isn't making a lot of sense, Alice, and he's saying some strange things."

"What like?" I ask, heart pounding.

"Oh, I don't know. Things about going to church – he hasn't been to church since he stopped living with his parents!" She tries to laugh. "And he'd been sitting on a swing, he said. He was sitting on a swing with one of the priests. And he was saying that line from the carol."

"The carol?"

"Yes, the holly one, you know."

The notes of the Saint Day carol drift into my mind, transporting me back to the harbourside. Why did I not call Mum and Dad when I thought of them earlier? I was too busy having a nice time sitting at the pub with Sophie. I should have been here with them, not let Mum go through all this on her own. I try not to read anything into the religious nature of Dad's strange hallucinations. "Did you tell anyone about this?"

"Yes, they said it's his fever." She sobs. "Why didn't I see the signs earlier?"

"Mum," I say softly, gently pressing her to sit down

and going to sit on the other chair in the room myself –
trying to gather my thoughts and feelings because I
think I am going to have to be the strong one in this
situation – "I could say the same myself. But when I left
yesterday, Dad was sitting up. And this morning he
was feeling much better."

"He said he was!" she wails.

"And I'm sure he was. You'd have known, if he was
feeling awful. These things can change, can't they?" I
say, as if I know anything. "You said yourself, you felt
worse in the mornings and evenings."

"But it was just a cold."

I can see there's not a lot I can do to comfort Mum
right now. We sit silently for a while.

"Do you know when they're bringing him back?" I
ask.

"It might be a while. They said they might have to
anaesthetise him, and they'll want to see he's
recovering OK before they bring him back down here."

It all sounds so serious. Well, it is, clearly, serious.

"Have you had anything to eat, Mum?"

"No, I – I'm not sure I'm hungry."

"I'll go and get something. You've got to keep your
own strength up." Now I really feel like I am talking to
an old lady.

"Ok love," she says in a small voice.

I find the same man who showed me to the room and
ask where I might find some vending machines. He
tells me but says the café might still be open for ten
minutes if I'd prefer something a bit more substantial.
I whizz through the corridors as politely as I can,
getting to the café with moments to spare. I pick up the

last two Chelsea buns, wrapped in cellophane and white paper; two bananas; a couple of cereal bars, and bottles of orange juice.

"Do you have time to make two coffees please?" I ask the kindly woman behind the counter.

"Just!" she smiles. "Are you going to be able to carry all of that?" She raises an eyebrow at the pile of snacks. Doesn't wait for an answer. "I'll get you a bag."

With the carrier bag in one hand and two coffees stacked in my other, I make slower progress back to Mum and again I rely on the lovely man on the ward, who spies me through the small, reinforced window on the door before I have to press the buzzer. I smile and thank him and go to find Mum. Dad's bed is still empty.

"Here you go," I say, my voice incongruously loud in the quiet space.

"Oh thank you, Alice."

"Just take the lid off first. The lady said it might be a bit too hot to drink straight away."

I sit down on the same chair as before.

Mum sends me a small smile. Takes the lid off her coffee and blows on it. Her look is faraway and I watch her for a moment, then I feel like I can actually see her determinedly pull herself together. She closes her eyes briefly, pulls her shoulders back. Looks at me.

"How was Holly's play? I don't think I even asked you about that."

"Oh Mum, it was lovely. Although – Holly forgot her lines!"

"Ah bless her, was she upset?"

"It was fine. Mrs Thomas prompted her and she carried on regardless. She thinks nobody noticed."

Mum smiles at this. "Good. And now it's the Christmas holidays," she says.

"Yep." I'm not feeling this small talk. I don't want it. We'll be talking about the weather next. "Dad reminded me, Mum, the other day, of that time I fell off the stage, when it was my play."

"Oh Alice," Mum's face comes alive at this memory. "You were so upset. Grandma and I had to dash backstage to come and comfort you. You were drowning out the action on stage!"

"Oh god!" I say, but I smile. "What a drama queen!"

"Ah no, you were so – well shocked, I suppose. And you'd hurt your ankle, and then you were so embarrassed. Bless you. We had to just get you home. You didn't want to stay for the encore!"

It's funny, thinking of me as a little girl, and how Mum would have felt about me the same way I do about Holly now. "And Dad wasn't there, was he?" I ask.

"No, he… well, Alice, I don't suppose we've ever really told you about that."

"About what?" I ask.

"That Christmas." Mum's eyes are glistening and she looks slightly faraway as she sends her mind back over the decades. "We tried to hide it from you."

"Hide what?"

"Well, your dad – he wasn't well that year, either."

"Really?" I don't remember that.

"Really." She sends me a serious look now and I see the Mum I know. "I suppose I could tell you about it now, if you like. Just until your dad gets back."

I nod, despite everything intrigued at the thought of

a time in my past I know nothing about. "Yes please, Mum. I'd like to know."

"We were about your age then, Alice. Your dad and me. Maybe a bit younger, I suppose. I was younger when I had you, wasn't I? And you were littler than Holly is now. It was your first year at school, and it was the year your Grandad – your dad's dad – died."

"Grandad," I say, my mind reaching for a memory just out of reach. An old man in my mind – he probably wasn't all that old in reality – kind and playful. Like my dad. I do have a vague memory of him letting me and my older cousins cover him in shaving foam. "He was lovely wasn't he, Mum?"

"He was a lovely man," she agrees. "And your dad was heartbroken when he died."

"I'm sure," I say, swallowing. Putting Dad into my shoes – or Sam's. My age. A young daughter. A sudden loss of a parent. Mum continues, latching on to the story, casting her mind back and glad of the focus; an alternative to just staring at an empty bed and waiting for news.

13.

Mum tells me that Dad had been away with work when Grandad died. At that time Dad was very focused on his career, and he'd not been great at visiting his parents. They hadn't minded; seen his ambition and also thought it only right that as a man he was intent on his work and providing for his family.

I don't actually remember Dad being like this really; in my mind Mum was the one with the career, who loved her job. Dad worked to live, he liked to say, while Mum lived to work and worked to live. "She does it all," Dad would say proudly, before she finally took retirement after her own spell of ill health.

Anyway, Dad had been on a training course when Grandma phoned my mum. I was out at school, it was my first term there, and I'd had some trouble settling in.

"Really?" I ask. I don't remember this either. My memories of primary school are rosy: a lovely, warm and welcoming place where I spent seven years with the same class of children, and we all knew each other inside out. I remember birthday parties and school trips, Christmas plays and summer discos. The rota for cleaning the fish tank in the junior two classroom. Winning a competition for drawing a plate of fish and chips – also in the junior two classroom, which seems a bit cruel now I think of it. Ringing the bell at the end of Friday afternoon assembly if it was your birthday. I loved that school.

"Oh yes, you weren't very happy at first. But you were so little. You seemed so small to me, Alice, much too tiny to be sending in to school. I could have kept you back but you were also so keen to learn and, well if I'm honest I wanted to get back to work full-time as well. I planned to do it the following January. It was only the first couple of weeks where you really resisted going in but it felt like forever to me. It was awful having to prise you off me in the mornings, and leave you crying. But they said you were alright after I'd left." She smiles at me. Manages to roll her eyes.

I dredge my memories. I do remember my first day, quite vividly: the other, taller children, and the arrangement of tables – which seemed so big but which I now realise would have been tiny, sized for little children. I remember clutching a bag of sweets on the way home with Mum, and I remember trays with shapes and blocks and coloured pens, and coloured paper. But I cannot remember ever being unhappy at that school.

"So what happened with Grandad? And Dad?" I prompt Mum, realising we've lost our focus. I glance at the clock. See I've already been at the hospital over an hour. Where is Dad? I try not to let my fears and imagination in. Mum returns to the story.

"Yes, your grandma phoned and I could tell straight away she was upset. She just came out with it. Your grandad had suffered a heart attack, and died. Just out of the blue." Mum struggles against a sob, maybe seeing the parallels with her own situation.

Grandma had not stayed on the phone long but Mum had managed to check she wasn't alone and no, her friend Doris was there with her. Mum promised to tell Dad and, slightly stunned, she phoned through to his office, because she had no contact details for the place where he was doing his training.

"Your dad used to call every lunchtime and every evening if he was away. He'd call every lunchtime regardless, while I was at home with you."

I do remember that, in the holidays, answering the phone at lunchtime and knowing it would be my dad. "Daddy!" I'd shout happily, feeling so proud to be able to answer the phone – knowing how to say the phone area code and our number.

"I thought you were your mum," he'd say every time. "You sound like a grown-up lady."

I would giggle and then I wouldn't know what to say. More often than not, Mum would be waiting next to me, smiling, and I'd hand her the phone without even saying bye.

I miss our old house now, suddenly, though I haven't really given it much of a thought in years. But that table under the stairs where we kept the phone – at that time a solid, blocky thing with the full dial of numbers. As I grew older we upgraded to a fancy wall-mounted number with buttons and I would wait for 6pm and pull the curly cord under the door to the dining room and talk to Julie for fifty-nine minutes at a time – anything after 6pm and under an hour was free – then she would call me back, and Mum and Dad would ask what on earth we had to talk about when we'd been together at school all day. Yet talk we did, and laugh, so much, until one or other of our parents had enough and maybe even needed to make their own phone calls.

On the day Grandma had called, it was one of the first times I'd gone into school if not happily then without any resistance, so Mum was feeling a bit happier. She'd had a busy morning and she'd made herself a tuna sandwich and a cup of tea, and was just settling down to eat her lunch and watch the news.

"I never did eat that sandwich, and the cup of tea went cold. I had to try and work out how to get hold of your dad. Obviously we didn't have mobile phones, and I'd never thought to get contact details for him. It was just a given that he would call me when he was free."

After Mum had got the number for the place Dad was training from secretary at his office, she called through and spoke to somebody on reception, then was left waiting for fifteen minutes while they went to get my dad. "That would have been an expensive phone call," she says, "not that it mattered, of course. Though we didn't have a lot in those days."

And Dad got to the phone, already knowing something must be wrong for Mum to have called him. "Is Alice OK?" was his first question apparently, and I feel my heart squeeze at the thought of this.

Mum had said yes, I was fine, then told him kindly that she did have some bad news and that his dad had died.

There had been a gasp and then silence, then she'd heard Dad crying. I find tears in my own eyes now at the thought of it, and of Dad being far from home, and Mum unable to see him or hold him.

"Come home, Phil," she had said and, like an obedient little boy, he said yes, he would.

Then had come an excruciating wait as Mum fretted that Dad shouldn't be driving in that state but he arrived home safely and she was finally able to hold him as she wanted to. And they came together to collect me from school – I think I do have a vague memory of this – and we went together to Grandma's house, which I don't remember at all. I suppose they shielded me from what was going on. I imagine being plonked in front of the TV with a beaker of squash and a biscuit while Mum and Dad looked after Grandma.

And I wasn't allowed to the funeral; it wasn't the done thing then, Mum tells me, to have children at funerals, so all of this is quite cloudy to me and to my shame I realise that I haven't thought enough about my parents losing their parents. I suppose it just felt, growing up, like the way things went, though I was really upset when Grandma died, as she'd been in our lives a lot and often looked after me when Mum and Dad were at work.

I suppose they probably shielded me from the worst of it, just as I've already tried to protect Ben and Holly from what's happening. Now, here in this otherworldly place, Mum is opening a door and letting some light fall onto their lives, their feelings, their struggles.

Dad was hit hard by his father's death. He and Grandad had been very close, and used to go to the football together, spend Sunday afternoons fishing. It had been the same since Dad was a boy and there seemed no reason to change this once he was married, and so he continued. Not selfishly but just in the way that was accepted, even expected, back then. Men worked hard during the week and deserved their weekend occupations.

Things did begin to change for Mum and Dad but at this time in their lives they were living as they'd been brought up. So anyway, when Grandad died, a gaping hole opened up for my dad and it seemed impossible to fill.

"Poor Dad," I say.

"I know. And your grandma too."

"Of course."

"But your grandma had a lot of friends around her, and some of them were already widows, though they weren't very old really. And they took her under their wings and kept her going."

"I remember those coach trips she used to go on!"

"Yes, we used to laugh at them but actually I think they were an important part of her life. She couldn't drive, and those trips took her to lots of different places, and with that big group of friends. I'm not for a minute saying she didn't miss your grandad. I know she did – he was a really lovely man – but suddenly she only had herself to think about. For probably the first time in her life."

I consider this. Freedom for Grandma, coming so late in life, when I had years of it in my twenties, once I'd ended things with Geoff of course. I should have made more of the opportunity, perhaps – gone travelling or something – but instead I settled into a steady, routine kind of life. Boring job, steady wage, regular hobbies. I suppose I didn't appreciate the value of the opportunities I had.

"But your dad," Mum continues, "well, he was so shocked. He hadn't seen it coming, at all. And he carried on – or tried to. Helped Grandma arrange the funeral, then went back to work the day after. For one thing, you didn't get much in the way of compassionate leave and for another I think he just wanted the normality, the routine of it all."

So Dad had tried to seek some kind of stability in work and ordinariness, just like I had done after Geoff.

"Anyway, I could see he wasn't himself, and of course he wouldn't be. And grief affects everyone differently. I know that now, having seen enough of it in my lifetime."

She swallows and I look away. I know what she is thinking and I'm thinking the same thing – will it be our turn next? "But I didn't have a very varied experience of it back then, I just knew your dad was so sad. He went off his food, though I tried really hard to make sure he was eating enough, and he went to work and came back, and barely spoke to me for a while. We were both miserable."

How had I missed this? I wonder. But of course, I was barely five years old.

"The one thing that made him smile was you," she says, looking at me. "He adored you, and he still does. Ben and Holly too."

That is enough to set my tears in motion. I think of Holly the other day, leaning into her grandad for comfort. Him singing that carol to her. And Ben, letting Dad hug him. "They both love him too. And you."

"I know they do. But Grandad's more fun isn't he? Sillier."

"Well that's true," I smile. "The sillier bit, at least. So what happened? Did Dad have counselling?"

"Did he heck! No, that kind of thing was definitely viewed as an indulgence back then. It wasn't anywhere near as common as it is now. No, your dad did as many men did – kept his mouth shut and carried on. Well, until… until he didn't."

"What do you mean?"

"Nothing dramatic," she hurries to reassure me. "No, he just – he didn't get up one day. He called in sick, which was something he would never normally do, and then he stayed in bed. I left him to it, I had to keep things going for you anyway, but he was the same the next day. And the one after."

"I really don't remember," I say.

"No. Well that's good, because we wouldn't have wanted you to. I think we told you Daddy was poorly and you accepted it because there was no reason not to. But I knew I couldn't let it carry on. You know me, Alice. On the Friday I think it was, once you were at school, I went back home and I made a pot of tea and I took it upstairs and made him sit up and made him talk to me. Which was not easy."

"It's not usually hard to get Dad talking," I try a little light humour.

"Not these days, no." Mum smiles. "But it was difficult then. Like I had to pull the words from him, and it was painful for us both. But it worked, and he opened up, and we talked about what we could do, and how I could help him, and that afternoon we both came to get you from school and we went for a walk and picked up some fish and chips on the way home. It wasn't all better of course, a long way from it, but it was a start."

Do I remember that afternoon? Or is my imagination stepping in now that Mum's told me about it?

"And it was you, and your grandma, that really got Dad back on track again. He started taking you swimming – and taking you to visit his mum at the weekends. I had to be a bit hard towards him about that because it felt like he couldn't quite see how lonely she was. How she might have been keeping busy but that didn't mean it was easy, and she was still heading home to an empty house at the end of the day."

The swimming I do remember, and the visits to Grandma's house. Making fudge with her – which totally failed and left us with a baking tray of very sweet gloop – going to the park near her house, playing in her garden with her neighbour's dog.

"It brought your dad closer to your grandma, which was the one good thing that came out of it all. And he was back at work, and you were happier at school, after the half-term break. I'd been dreading you going back, thinking you'd kick up a stink, but you were absolutely fine, and life felt a little bit more settled. And they started talking about the Christmas play, and suddenly you were besotted with school and you wanted to practise your lines every night, which your dad did with you. And you and he used to sing *Little Donkey*, do you remember? You really loved that song. In fact, you wanted a donkey of your own for quite a long time."

"I still do."

"Well at least it wouldn't be up to me to muck it out these days," she smiles. "And then, we all got ill."

Oh yes. It began with me. Lots of the children in my class had been off, and my teacher too, and then I began to have a sore throat, and earache, and a runny nose, and a high temperature…

"I don't think I'd known you to be that poorly before," Mum says, "so I was a bit worried, and I took you to the doctor and I remember he was really snotty with me and said it was just a virus and to get you to have some of those soluble painkillers, which of course you hated, and you were off school for a week, and so worried about missing the play. It sounds strange maybe but you being ill also helped your dad as it really brought his focus in to you and at the same time he started thinking about Christmas, and I was really pleased when he said he was going to invite Grandma. I had suggested it a while before then but he hadn't been in the right place to think about it. So as you began to feel better, we were able to look ahead a bit more and we knew that Christmas would be a really tough one, but also that we needed to make sure that it was magical for you, and that Grandma wouldn't be on her own. It was one thing to have friends around her in normal times but that Christmas week, people tend to be busy with their own families, and all the usual things like groups she went to wouldn't be on. I think that can be the worst, longest week of the year, you know," Mum says, her eyes filling with tears.

"Oh Mum. It's going to be OK," I say, though I have no idea if that's true. How can I know that? We're both aware that I can't. I spy a nurse walking past the window. "Shall I just go and find out if there's an update?"

I know there won't be, but I think Mum needs a break and I want to feel useful, somehow.

"Excuse me," I say and the nurse turns.

"Yes?" She smiles at me.

"I'm Phil – Phillip – Griffiths' daughter–" I gesture to the room I've just come out of, see Dad's name on the board outside – "Mum and I are just waiting to hear if there's any news."

"I haven't heard anything yet," she says. "Once a patient's off the ward they're out of our hands but I'll see if I can find out what's happening."

"Thank you," I say, and shuffle apologetically back to Mum. I don't like bothering the no doubt overworked staff here, but at the same time this is my dad, and we need to be able to ask questions.

"Nothing," I say to Mum.

"I know. They'll tell us when there's news," she says. "Look, pull your chair over here would you, Alice? It seems daft you sitting the other side of the bed when Dad's not even in it."

I do as she suggests, and I lean against her, grateful for my mum's arm around my shoulder. Just hours ago, I was doing the same with Sophie, outside the Mainbrace. I think briefly, self-pityingly, of how everything looked different then. I was just looking forward to Christmas. But that is a pointless train of thought to follow. I close my eyes for a while, breathing in my mum's familiar smell; the perfume she has always worn, and washing powder she has always used, which create her own unique scent, and which transport me back to my childhood as she continues the story of that Christmas so long ago.

"Just as you started to get better, I got ill," she laughs. "It was pretty much par for the course, to be honest. But that too made your dad stronger as he could see I was really struggling and so he arranged to work from home – a very unusual thing in those days – for the week and he was working in the dining room, in between taking you to school, bringing me Lemsips and cups of tea, and of course collecting you again – then looking after you in the afternoon, making tea, putting you to bed, and working into the evening.

I was so tired and so grateful but I hadn't realised it was like the flipside of his grief. I think, looking back now, it was all a bit manic. At the time I was just happy to see him moving again and energetic. But I don't think it was a surprise when he started to feel a bit ill too. However, by that point we were not far away from Christmas and he'd already been at home for a week, even though he was working, so he ignored it and downplayed how awful he felt. Thankfully I was on the mend so I was able to start doing school runs, and all the usual chores, and your dad could get back to the office."

"This all sounds so familiar," I say, thinking of how hard it can be to manage everything with a young family and how either Sam or I being ill is a huge inconvenience, to say the least. There just isn't time for us to be ill. I can well imagine Mum and Dad's predicament, without the added complication of grief as well. "I do wonder sometimes how we manage."

"You and Sam have a lot on your plate, with Holly–" Mum says – "and you do a wonderful job."

"Thank you, Mum. I didn't really mean just me and Sam. I mean all of us. Parents."

"I suppose when you were little it was quite common for one parent to work while the other took on the household responsibilities. Yes, more often than not that would be the mum. But you know things changed in that respect for me and Dad, a bit. But even so, for your generation, everyone is working and trying to achieve so much for your kids. Taking them to clubs here, there and everywhere. Days out, expensive holidays. On top of both parents working. I have so much admiration for you all. It is lovely that you all want to do so much. But it must be exhausting."

"Yes," I say, resting my head against her shoulder. "It is a bit."

I have avoided trying to do too much with Ben and Holly. Swimming is a must but anything else is optional. I do sometimes feel lacking in that respect but I also tell myself to stand firm. I don't want to wear my children, or myself, out. And managing Holly's medical stuff is hard-going. Every three days we have to do a full change of insulin, cannula, etc, and I can tell you it isn't getting a whole lot easier. Sometimes she really, really doesn't want to do it and it's worse at the moment because it's cold and I think her skin is more sensitive. It clearly hurts when the cannula goes in and it sends my stomach tumbling each time, makes me feel sick, but I have to make it happen. Every ten days we change her sensor, again a painful process, physically for Holly and emotionally for me. These things should never be an excuse not to do other stuff, but it does all take its toll. I think it's important that we take life as easily as we can but that doesn't stop me feeling like I'm letting the side down sometimes.

"Anyway, your dad and I certainly felt like we had enough on our plates, but we knew your grandma needed some support, and your dad was absolutely determined to get her over to us for Christmas. And he wanted her to see you in your play as well. He was so excited about it! So he booked the afternoon off work and he drove to Grandma's house."

"Even though he was ill?"

"Even though he was ill," she confirms. "And he picked her up but apparently she was flapping a bit about what to bring and by the time they left it was snowing."

"Uh-oh," I say.

"Yes. Uh-oh. And it started to stick. And they got as far as the big hill, and your dad's car started to slide, and Grandma was panicking, and your dad was trying not to, but apparently she was shrieking and he had to really shout at her to get her to stop."

"Oh dear."

"Yes. It didn't go down well but anyway, she could see he was doing his best, and other cars were slipping too, and Dad did the best thing he could think of, which was to pull up on the hill, and hope nobody slid into the car. And then they were stuck."

"I had no idea about any of this!"

"No, I suppose it just blended into the past for us. I mean, at the time it was quite dramatic but as you know, your dad and your grandma were OK."

"Wasn't Grandma there at the play?" I ask. She and Mum brought me home after my accident. I know that.

"Yes! Well remembered."

"So where was Dad?"

I think back to the feeling of excitement in the classroom before the play began. It's possible these memories are getting mixed up with those from other years but it's all so vivid. The long rank of classroom windows steaming up as the air outside grew colder and the sky grew darker, and in the stuffy warmth we were pulling off school uniforms, those unbearably thick tights with the low crotches, and pulling on our costumes, transforming into inn-keepers, shepherds, Kings, Mary, Joseph… even a donkey and a sheep. It felt so late and so thrilling, not to have gone home. This on top of the novelty of eating lunch in a hall which had a huge Christmas tree in the corner and a stage set up at one end. That hall seemed enormous back then. And the Christmas holidays were approaching… the teachers probably at their wits' end, just trying to keep us busy and themselves from losing it. We seemed to spend quite a lot of time creating paperchains and making paper snowflakes, from what I recall. And I loved bringing home little piles of Christmas cards addressed only to me – not to Mum and Dad as well.

Those Christmases are so vivid in my mind, trees a jumble of shiny, multi-coloured baubles, handmade decorations and gaudy tinsel. Every year, Dad would try out the fairy lights and curse the bulbs which weren't working, muttering something about the fuse, which I had absolutely no interest in. Presents were wrapped in bright, thin paper, and I can still conjure up the excitement of Christmas morning, waking to find that Father Christmas had been and feeling those little packages crackling and rustling, crammed tightly into one of Dad's old rugby socks which doubled as a stocking.

With the remembered taste of paperchain glue on my tongue, I turn with a start and pull away from Mum as the nurse I had spoken to knocks on the door and enters the room.

"I've just spoken to the team Mr Griffiths is with and they've finished their tests. They are just reviewing the results, and we should have some news shortly."

"Thank you," I say.

"Thank you," says Mum.

We look at each other, and I realise I'm shaking. I see that Mum is too.

"Shall I get us another drink?" I ask.

"I'll bring you one," the nurse says kindly. "Tea?"

"That would be so kind," says Mum. "Thank you."

"Milk? Sugar?"

"Just milk please," we say in unison.

She laughs. "Coming right up."

We are quiet for a while, lost in our own thoughts and memories and worries. When the nurse returns she brings not only two cups of tea but a small plate of chocolate biscuits. "We've got far too many." She smiles. "You'll be doing us a favour if you have these."

We both thank her again.

Nibbling a biscuit, I prompt Mum to continue the story, hoping to take her mind and mine away from contemplating what news we might receive, "So if Grandma made it to the play and Dad didn't, what happened?"

"Your Grandma got a lift."

"What…? How?"

"A couple of local farmers with snow ploughs volunteered to clear the roads. They managed to get part way up the hill, but it got too steep. But they walked up to the stranded cars to see if anyone was vulnerable. Your dad waved them over and said that his mum was, and one of the farmers got her to his tractor and brought her to our house."

"No!"

"Yes! He was lovely, actually."

"But what about Dad?" I want to know. "He was ill, wasn't he? Wouldn't that make him vulnerable?"

"Yes but of course he didn't mention that! There was a lady with a little toddler in another car, and he insisted they took the other place in the tractor, and he started to walk."

"He walked home? All the way? In the snow? Even though he was ill?" I can hardly believe what I'm hearing. That hill is a long way from where we lived – a good few miles.

"He did," Mum confirms. "Carrying Grandma's bags too. And Grandma arrived with me and we had no idea what he was doing, or how or when he would be back, but it was nearly time for your play and we had to go. It wasn't even all that snowy at home!"

"Oh wow, and I thought Holly's birth was the most dramatic Christmas we'd had."

"It was certainly eventful," Mum says.

"So you came to the play, with Grandma…" I prompt.

"Yes, we came, and saw you do your thing, and then saw you vanish, and heard the thump as you hit the floor. My god Alice, my nerves were already frayed, wondering what had happened to your dad!"

"But I was alright. And so was dad?"

"Well, yes, you were, and he was. He got home later – much later – having walked most of the way and then hitching a lift the last couple of miles."

"Dad hitched a lift?" I ask, incredulous.

"Yes, and he got back just as we were sitting down to tea. I don't know if I've ever been so glad to see him!"

"So what did you do before he got home? You just carried on as if nothing had happened?"

"I didn't know what to do, Alice. I was scared. But you were shattered, and a bit shaken still from your fall from grace–" she allows herself a small smile at this although it quickly turns back to a frown as she remembers – "and your grandma was worn out, of course. I was trying to keep her calm too. I had no way of contacting your dad and I just had to hope for the best. I hoped he hadn't decided to sleep in the car, although the state he was in when he arrived at home, maybe that would have been better. His poor red, soaked feet… of course he'd gone to Grandma's straight from work so he was wearing his office shoes, and his suit. He did at least have a coat and hat and gloves in the car, but he was so cold and wet. Shivering like nobody's business. I sometimes wonder if that's why he became so susceptible to chest infections and then of course to Covid. I made him go straight upstairs and ran him a warm bath – it couldn't be too hot but enough to warm him up – then put him to bed. And I called the out of hours GP, who came and checked him over. Nothing untoward, he said. Nothing bed-rest and paracetamol wouldn't fix."

And I do remember now, that Christmas that Dad
was ill. But I had no idea about any of this, or what
lengths he had gone to in order to make sure his mum
was OK, and that we were all together. I had just been
annoyed at him for missing my play.

14.

I nibble one of the chocolate biscuits as I think back over the story Mum has just told. And then she says she needs the loo, and I take the opportunity to check my phone.

Sam: **Any news?**

Sophie: **I hope Phil is OK. Thinking of you xxx**

Sam: **Mummy this is Holly. When r u coming hom.**

That at least makes me smile, though it also pulls at my heartstrings a little. I type out a quick reply, though I suspect she may be in bed by now:

Hi Sam, Ben and Holly. I am with Grandma at the moment and Grandad is just having some tests done so I will stay till we get the results. I miss you and love you and wish I was home but Grandma doesn't want to be alone. She sends her love too xxx

To Sophie:

Thank you Sophie, it was lovely to get your message.

Just waiting for some test results for Dad. Wishing we were back at the Mainbrace drinking cider! It was a lovely afternoon, thank you xx

Then Mum returns and I see her looking into the room hopefully, as if Dad might have returned or at the very least there will be somebody there to give us some news. Disappointment is written all over her face.

"Sit down, Mum, we'll hear something soon."

"It's late, Alice. I don't think you should stay much longer."

"Mum! I am not leaving you here until we know what's going on. I want to know how Dad is as well, you know."

"Of course you do, sorry. But Sam and the kids will be missing you."

"They will be alright," I say firmly. "And they have Sophie there too."

"Of course! How is she? Have you found out why she's come to you for Christmas?"

"I think she just wanted to spend it with Sam," I say, and leave it at that.

"I can understand that. What about her boyfriend?"

"I don't think he's too bothered about spending Christmas with Sam."

"That's not what I meant and you know it!" I am gratified to have at least raised a smile from her.

But both our heads swivel then, at the sound of somebody at the door.

"Mrs Griffiths and… Alice, is it?" A woman I haven't seen before comes into the room. She is smartly dressed, with a stethoscope round her neck.

"Oh yes, Doctor…" Mum has clearly forgotten her name.

"Doctor Surani," the woman says kindly. "How are you both? I am sorry you've been left for so long. We've had a bit of a build-up upstairs, everyone wanting their tests before Christmas." She smiles, but she knows we're not here for chit-chat. "Anyway, we have run the tests we needed on your husband, Mrs Griffiths, and we do think he has a severe chest infection, which has sent his immune system into overdrive, and why he has developed sepsis."

She speaks so matter-of-factly, yet gently. But sepsis… I know it can be treated but I also know it can be fatal.

"But is he OK? Can we see him? When are you bringing him back?" Mum can't seem to stem the flow of questions.

"Mrs Griffiths… I am afraid Mr Griffiths needs some help breathing at the moment."

"He…?" Mum flounders, searching for the words she needs.

"He needs to be on a ventilator," Doctor Saruni clarifies. "And for this he needs to be on a different ward."

"Can we see him?" I ask this time.

"You can," she confirms. "But he is under heavy sedation. And I have to explain this carefully to you, that Mr Griffiths is in critical care right now. We have had to intubate to use the ventilator and this is, in effect, a form of life support."

I feel sick. Life support? I visualise images from TV programmes I've seen, and films: of patients attached to beeping, bleeping machines. And, inevitability, the crunch decision.

"It's not necessarily as you are imagining." Dr Saruni continues. "But it will be difficult to see your husband… your dad… like this, so please try to prepare yourselves. Right now, Mr Griffiths needs this assistance. He is also on a drip to help combat the sepsis."

Mum's mouth is a tight line. I know she is trying hard to keep her emotions in check. I am struggling myself, so many possible scenarios flying through my mind.

"Can you take us to him?" I ask.

"I will ask Georgia to. I have to visit another patient now," says Dr Saruni. "But I will come and see you before the end of my shift. And you will be in very good hands in CCU."

So it is CCU, I think. To me, with my limited knowledge of hospitals, that is the last place you want to be. Because you know if you are there you are in a very serious position. Mum catches my eye, no doubt thinking the same thing.

Dr Saruni lays a kind hand on her shoulder then, briefly, on my arm. "I'll get Georgia," she says, and she leaves the room, an air of crisp, authoritative efficiency accompanying her.

I look at Mum and she looks at me, and collapses into my arms.

"Mrs Griffiths?" A young woman knocks on the still-open door.

We both look up.

"I'm Georgia. Dr Saruni has asked me to take you up

to your husband. Would you like to come with me?"

Picking up our bags and Dad's coat, which was on the back of Mum's chair, we follow Georgia obediently, and she talks to us so kindly it could make me cry. It is strange to think that the room we were in will be stripped and cleaned and soon a new patient will be installed there. As we go along the corridors, I find myself wanting to rip down the tinsel that adorns the pictures created and donated by local artworks. To push that row of seats over. Send that empty trolley bed skidding down the corridor. I have so much pent-up anger, but I push it down. Back into its own little box. It will have to stay quiet and wait.

It is way past visiting hours now. There is a hush about the place so that the sound of our footsteps rings off the hallway walls and Mum and I answer Georgia's questions quietly, telling her about Ben and Holly, and Holly's play, knowing full well that she is trying to keep us calm and take our minds off the situation at hand, but allowing her to do so.

"Here we are." We stop outside a set of double doors. "I'm afraid I have to ask you to turn your phones off before we go in," says Georgia, "because of the nature of some of the machines in here. And we definitely need to hand-sanitise."

I take my phone from my pocket, seeing Julie has messaged. Oh god, I hope she is OK too. But I don't have time to check what she's sent now. Hopefully just a good moan about when the baby is finally going to arrive. Reluctantly, I switch my phone off and apply a good helping of sanitiser to my hands, Mum doing the same with hers, and then Georgia buzzes us in, taking us to the desk and explaining who we are. "This is Jane," she says. "She'll look after you from here. Take care of yourselves, and each other."

"We will," I say. "Thank you." Then, "Merry Christmas." Those words don't sound right – there is nothing merry about this – but Georgia smiles.

"And the same to you."

I am doing my utmost to hold it together, for Mum and for myself. Jane leads the way to Dad's room and tells us what we can expect, trying to prepare us as Dr Saruni did too, but I don't think anything could really have primed us for the sight that greets us.

There is my dad, in a hospital gown, in a hospital bed, a tube leading from a mask which is fitted over his face, attaching him to a machine which is helping him breathe; an oxygen monitor clipped to his finger, and a drip attached via to a cannula in the back of his hand.

Mum emits a half-gasp, half-sob, and I catch my breath. Jane lays a hand on Mum's arm.

"I can't say I know how you feel," she says, "but please be assured that Mr Griffiths is in the best place here. We can provide the support he needs while his body fights the infection. And our visiting hours are less strict here than the rest of the hospital so you can come and go as you need to, pretty much, but we do ask you not to come in if you are ill yourselves, and it can be a good idea to call ahead. But you're here now so please take a seat and make yourselves as comfortable as you can. One of the ICU doctors will be here shortly and they can tell you a bit more information."

As it happens it's another three hours until a doctor is available. In that time, we gaze at Dad through tired, disbelieving eyes. I catch myself dropping off a number of times, experiencing strange, semi-waking dreams and shaking myself awake. Mum does fall asleep at one point and I put Dad's coat over her to try and keep her warm and dozing. No point in us both staying awake.

Jane comes in every hour to check Dad's vitals and make some notes, and each time she smiles and says he is 'steady' but she can't, or won't, say more than that.

But when the doctor arrives at the door I gently put my hand on Mum's arm and say her name. She takes a moment to come round then clearly registers quickly where we are.

"Hello, Mrs Griffiths." The doctor shakes her hand. "I'm Dr Cooper. And you must be the daughter?" He turns to me. I'm not all that keen on 'the daughter' but really I am too tired and too worried for Dad to care.

"That's me," I confirm. "The daughter."

Despite everything, I see Mum shoot me a look.

"OK, well I apologise for having taken so long to get to you but we have had something of an emergency. The nature of the work, I'm afraid."

I wonder what sights he has just seen, and I notice now the tired shadows under his eyes and feel sorry for my abrasiveness. His is a hard job.

"So I don't know how much you have been told but right now we have Mr Griffiths on an IV drip of antibiotics to fight off the sepsis, and on a ventilator to keep him breathing. His oxygen levels are satisfactory, but there is room for improvement. He'll be fed by tube for the time being."

I picture a tube going into Dad's mouth, like a drinking straw, but I know enough to understand that it could be done by a pump not too dissimilar to Holly's.

"Will he get better?" I ask, feeling like a child.

"We have every hope that he will. But of course there are no guarantees. I do understand how worried you must be. And I'm aware of the stigma of CCU but believe me, we do have patients leaving to make perfectly good recoveries."

I soften towards him even further.

"How long will he be sedated for?" asks Mum.

"As long as he needs to be," says Dr Cooper. "I am aware that is not the answer you want but I can't be any more exact than that. Please believe me though, Mrs Griffiths, we have an excellent team here. The best in the hospital, in my opinion. Jane will take great care of you and at seven she will hand over to one of her colleagues, who is just as excellent."

Seven am, I think. It's within touching distance now and I haven't slept. And I realise with a jolt that it's past midnight. It's Christmas Eve.

I feel suddenly terribly homesick and I just want to be in bed with Sam, and with Ben and Holly tucked in beside us, though I absolutely know Ben wouldn't stand for that these days. I want to wind back the clock a few days, stop it in a better time. Maybe Saturday lunchtime at the pub. That was a nice day.

My stomach churns and I know Mum must be feeling twice as bad. So I sit up straight and say thank you to Dr Cooper and that we know Dad is in good hands here. The doctor, who must be about my age; maybe with a family at home, smiles at me, but I think I see sadness in his eyes. I just don't know if it's for us specifically, or for everything and everyone he has seen throughout his work.

After the doctor has left, Mum and I sit in quiet contemplation for a while.

Then, "Did you take in what he said, Alice?"

I look at her. "I think so."

"Good. I feel so confused and scared by it all. I might need you to remind me."

"Of course, Mum."

"But love, I want you to go home now."

"No Mum, I can't."

"You can, and you must. Your family need you. It's Christmas, and Holly's birthday tomorrow. She and Ben will want their mum at home."

"I don't want to leave you and Dad," I say in a small voice. The thought of leaving them here like this rips into me.

"I know. But there is nothing you can do, or that I can do, for that matter. But you're going to be exhausted, and you can't let this ruin Christmas. Santa still has to come and see that good boy and girl. And they're still going to wake up at some godforsaken hour. And you've got us all coming to—"

She realises that I won't have all of them coming anymore. That Dad certainly won't be there and it's unlikely she will be either.

"One day at a time, Mum," I say gently, as much for my own benefit as hers. The thought of cooking a Christmas dinner for everyone is overwhelming; impossible, imagining trying to put a brave, jolly face on and actually celebrate not just Christmas but my daughter's birthday, though I know I must. I imagine how hard it must have been for Dad, walking home through the snow that day, and how much strength he must have had to summon. For his mum, for my mum, and for me.

"I'd better phone Sam at least," I say to Mum now. "He'll be wanting to know what's happening."

I walk the empty corridors alone, the windows either side filled with the darkness of the night, overhead lights turned down to an eerie glow. I'm glad to reach the ground floor where A&E is incredibly busy and quite noisy too, but at least there is life here.

Outside, the ground is sparkly with frost, the moon a fingernail curve in the sky. On any other Christmas Eve morning, I would see the magic in this but it is hard, if not impossible, to feel that right now.

"Alice?" Sam picks up on the first ring and I know he will have been barely able to sleep himself. I picture him in our bed, and I want more than anything to be there with him. Hiding in the darkness. But there are times when life asks something of us and I know that this is one such time for me. I cannot hide.

Pacing up and down the path, I fill Sam in on what's been happening. He is quiet, listening, no doubt worried himself.

"What are you going to do, Alice? Do you want to stay with your mum?"

"I don't know. I mean, yes of course I do, but she's insisting I come home. Says I need to be with you and Ben and Holly and Sophie. She is so tired, Sam. I don't know how she's going to cope with this."

"She will, Alice. Whatever – whatever happens. We'll make sure of it, won't we?"

"Yes," I smile slightly, relieved to hear Sam's words – the 'we' that reminds me we are a team, and I am not alone.

"I'll come and get you whenever you want me to."

"I know. Thank you. And I really want to come home, but it's the middle of the night. Well, kind of. You can't leave the kids."

"Sophie's here…"

"I know, but it's not fair on her, and she won't know what to do if there's a problem with Holly."

That's my main concern really; what if Sam comes out to get me and Holly has a hypo? Realistically, he will only be out a couple of hours – but what if there was a problem with the car, or we have a crash on the way back? I know it sounds silly and dramatic, and like I'm a terrible pessimist, but these are the what ifs and right now things seem so precarious – life seems so fragile – that I don't want to take any risks.

"I'll stay till it's light. Get Mum some breakfast, and you can have yours, then maybe you can come and get me, about half-eight?"

"Of course I can. I can do whatever you want. Just say the word."

"Thank you, Sam. I love you so much."

"I love you too, Alice. Take care. And give your folks my love. You know I love them too." His voice breaks a little on these last words, and I only love him more for it.

I decide to take a moment or two for myself. I feel like my head's been spinning with all that has gone on and it will do me good to breathe. Though I am not so sure I want to be in this particular moment, thinking of Lizzie's mindful advice. This is not a time I can cherish.

Despite the cold, I sit down on a bench and think how I am right in the heart of it now, where lives begin and lives end. Where people might leave in excited anticipation, or heart-stopping agony.

Somewhere deep inside that building are my mum and my dad, and around them other little bubbles of people, all living out their own lives' dramas. I will go back in for a while but then I must go home. I know it is right, and I know Mum wants me to, but I will feel awful leaving her and Dad behind. But it's Christmas Eve. I'm as tired as can be but it's time to get back to my family and make the magic happen for my children just as Mum and Dad always did for me.

Just before I go back inside, I remember I had a message from Julie. I click onto it and start at her words:

Alice! Where are you? I've been trying to call. SWITCH YOUR PHONE ON GODDAMMIT! It's started, my waters have broken. I'm going in! See you on the other side xxx

15.

I don't tell Mum immediately about Julie's message. It sounds silly but I don't know if it is appropriate somehow but then I think, she will want to know.

"Oh Alice, oh my goodness, what timing! To think she's giving birth while all this is happening. It just shows how life goes on regardless." Mum's eyes are shining and I just love her so much, and her ability to think truly of others. Even when her own world is threatening to fall apart, these feelings for Julie are strong and genuine.

Now my head really is spinning, at the thought that Julie will have her baby soon, all being well. Or maybe she's already had it. I have no way of knowing. And maybe, just maybe, things will turn a corner here. I can't help staring at Dad, willing him to open his eyes, even though I know that's just not going to happen. He is out for the count, as he should be. I imagine how scary it would be, waking to find a tube down your throat and your arm hooked up to a machine.

"Sam's coming about half eight," I say.

"That's still a while off, love." Mum looks concerned.

"I know, but it's fine. I don't want him waking the kids up. And I want to be here with you, in case – in case anything happens."

"It already feels like this nightmare's been going on forever," she says.

"I think you should get some more sleep, Mum. While I'm here to keep an eye on Dad. See if you can, please, or you won't be able to function. I can get a few hours when I'm back home."

"With those excited children? On Christmas Eve? Good luck with that!" She smiles but I can see she is tempted by the idea of sleep.

"Go on, Mum, close your eyes. Just see if you drop off."

Pulling Dad's coat up all the way to her neck, her surreptitious inhale doesn't go unnoticed by me and I know she's just taking in the smell of him. I keep an eye on her as she closes her eyes and her head begins to loll. Just like I did, she catches herself out a couple of times, but then she gives in to the need and she is soon snoring gently.

Now I have time to myself again – in a way, at least. Aside from the regular check-ins from Jane, who is kind and gentle and asks if I'm OK but demands no more conversation from me, I am left to my own thoughts. And my mind drifts back to Mum's story, of how Dad walked all that way through the snow to get home. And how I'd been cross with him for not getting to my play! I know I was just a child, and had no idea of the lengths he'd gone to, in order to make sure Grandma was OK, and to try not to miss my big moment on stage, but it still makes me feel guilty. I remember telling Sophie, though, that she can't blame herself for how she acted when she was eleven, and I certainly can't worry about how I behaved when I wasn't even five years old.

But I want him to know now, how much I love him. How much I appreciate everything he has done for me throughout my life, and not just for me but my children too. How much we all love him. I want to tell him, make sure he really, truly knows. Oh it hurts, all this. Seeing him so helpless. But Dr Cooper said he could make a perfectly good recovery. He did say that, didn't he? I have to just hope, against hope. I lean my head back against the chair and without meaning to I doze off too. When I wake it's to Jane checking in and I strain to remember my dreams but they remain frustratingly out of reach.

"What time is it?" I whisper.

"It's half six. I'll be handing over shortly, to my colleague Estella. She's Spanish and lovely. And an excellent nurse."

"Thanks so much. Will you be on shift tonight again?" I ask, not sure if I want to see her again or not. Because if I do, that means Dad's still in the ICU. But if I don't see her, what would that mean – that Dad's recovering on a different ward, or – no, I can't even think that thought.

"I will," she smiles, "all the way to Christmas morning."

"Ah – and do you have somebody to look after you on Christmas Day?"

"Yes, my husband's got it all covered. I get home, have a nap, and then wake up for presents and lunch."

"You can't have much sleep."

"No, but at least we don't have kids yet so I can have another nap in the afternoon if I want to. I can't wait!" she smiles. "But I will probably see you tonight. You should get some sleep today if you can."

"I'll try my best."

When Estella comes in to introduce herself, I wake Mum as I know she will want to meet her. I then go in search of breakfast because it won't be long now till Sam gets here. I go back to the shop where I bought the snacks and coffee last night, and it's the same lady on duty. I think she recognises me, but she must see so many faces, she might just be being kind.

"Long night?" she asks.

"Yes, really long."

"Coffee?" she asks.

"Yes, most definitely. And I'll take some pastries as well please, and a couple of orange juices. Thank you."

We still have the bananas I bought last night, which will give Mum some energy during the day. And I'll go to the bungalow sometime and pick up some of the things she needs. I feel grubby and unwashed myself, after a night fully clothed. The least Mum could do with is a set of fresh clothes and a toothbrush.

I take the coffees back up to Dad's room, struck by how used I already am to seeing him prostrate and unconscious in his bed. This time yesterday there is no way I could even have imagined this.

"Thank you Alice," says Mum.

"You are very welcome. Now are you sure you don't want me to stay today?"

"Honestly Alice, I will feel much better to know you're with your family."

"You're my family too, Mum."

"You know what I mean." Mum smiles.

I imagine a time in the future, when my children might have their own children, and I will have to put my own feelings and needs aside for the good of them.

Will it feel strange, like these days of them being so little and dependent on me were just yesterday, or do parents get used to not being of such vital importance as their children grow up?

"I will come back later," I say firmly.

"We'll see how it goes…"

"Mum!" I am outraged. "As if I'm not going to come back and see you and Dad later."

"Sorry, Alice. I think I'm doing you a favour, trying not to put the pressure on. Of course you'll want to come back. But just remember, if Holly or Ben need you, you put them first, OK?"

"OK," I say, knowing there is no way I'm not coming back.

We sip our coffees and I insist Mum has her pastry and that I leave mine with her for later.

"I'll get something on the way back," I say, my mind going unbidden to the McDonald's we'll be passing on the way home.

And then it's twenty past eight and it's time to go, and it is incredibly hard. I don't want to leave Mum to deal with everything, and I don't want to leave Dad, in case…

"I'll call you, Alice. If anything happens, I'll call," promises Mum. And we hug, and both cry a little bit, but being made of strong stuff we both also step back, wipe our eyes, try to smile.

"Bye Mum," I say, and I turn and leave, waiting till I've exited through the double doors before allowing my tears to stream freely down my face.

I'm in for a surprise in the car park though. There is not only Sam, Ben and Holly in our car, but Sophie too. And behind them is another car, containing Karen and Ron.

Ben and Holly are waving at me and I wave back, desperate to see them and hold them, feel their very warm, very real and very alive bodies pressed to me, but Sophie gets out of the car first, brandishing a bag.

"Hello," I say, hugging her. "You're up early."

"I can get up before eight when I have to, you know," she grins. "Look, we got some things for your mum." She opens the bag so I can see a brand-new packet of underwear, and a deodorant, a toothbrush and toothpaste, as well as a puzzle book, a novel, some bags of nuts, some satsumas, and a bar of Galaxy.

"Oh Sophie, that's so lovely."

"And Granny Karen wants to go and see her. Do you think – do you think that would be OK?"

Karen, perhaps hearing her name, comes to join us. "I don't want to interfere," she says, hugging me. "But Sam said you were worried about leaving Sue on her own and I just thought – I can either sit in with her so somebody can keep an eye on Phil while she sleeps or gets some fresh air, or else I can sit and read my book in the café and if she needs anything she can let me know."

Sam comes to join us, wrapping me in a huge hug, pressing his face to my ear. "Is that OK? I couldn't stop her." Louder he says, "The shopping was Mum's idea."

"That is so thoughtful of you, Karen. Thank you so much. Mum will be really touched."

"I just thought you might rest easier, too, if you know

there's somebody else on hand. And I can call you, if
Sue can't get out of the room, or – well, I don't know."
Karen actually looks quite unsure of herself, and I feel
a warmth flood through me. I step forward and
envelop my mother-in-law in the biggest hug I've ever
given her. "That is really kind of you, thank you Karen,
and I am sure Mum would be really happy to know you
are here."

I hope I'm right but even if Mum's not 100% on this,
my mind will be more at ease if I know she is not alone.
I tell Karen where to find her and she heads off on her
mission.

"Thank you, Ron." I wave at him and he issues a
salute. "Take care, and get some rest, Alice," he calls
out of his window. "I've got Poppy back here and I'm
taking her for a walk."

"Really?"

Ron, a retired vet, is perhaps the best person I could
imagine to take care of Poppy – and in doing so he's
removing one item from my list of things to do today. I
am so tired, all this kindness will have me on my knees.
It certainly has me close to tears.

"I could do with the exercise, Alice. And I can work
up an appetite for Christmas dinner."

My heart sinks then as I remember again all the effort
and energy it's going to take to keep Christmas going.

"That's another thing," Sam says, as though reading
my mind. "We don't have to cook tomorrow."

"Of course we do. It's Christmas! It's Holly's
birthday!"

"Well, I spoke to Christian and he's working all day
tomorrow. I explained the situation to him and he said

we can either go to the Cross Section and they'll squeeze us in – whenever works for us, somehow – or, if we don't feel like eating out, he's going to deliver dinner to our door."

"Are you kidding?" I ask, elated despite my exhaustion.

"Would I joke about something like that? I mean, I know you love cooking, but…"

"Ha ha. But what about Holly? I mean, it's her birthday, will she mind us changing the plans?"

"Are you kidding? Chris told her she's going to have a Christmas birthday throne if we eat in the restaurant and now she's absolutely full of it."

At that moment the back doors of the car open. "Mummy, why are you taking so long?"

Holly and then Ben rush to me, hugging me tightly.

"How did you two escape your seats?" I ask, laughing.

"I did it," says Ben. "It's easy."

"Can we see Grandad?" Holly asks.

"Not right now my love, he's not very well."

"But Granny Karen's seeing him."

"Yes, well she's an adult," I say and I'm relieved to see she accepts my flimsy reasoning.

"And these two are going to Natalie's later, to watch… *Elf*!"

"Bobby and Courtney have never seen it!" exclaims Ben.

"No way," I say, shepherding my children back towards the car. "We'd better go, we must have used up our twenty minutes' grace. Sophie, you go in the front."

"Are you sure?"

"Yes, I want to snuggle up with these two."

And squeeze though it is, between Holly's car seat and Ben's booster, I am just so happy to be here, right in the heart of my thoughtful, fantastic family, who have somehow worked together to rub at least some of my worries away. Even so, as Sam starts the car and we head out towards the main road, my children already bickering across me like I'm not even there, I can't help but take one look back at the hospital and wonder what it has in store for us.

16.

Somehow, thanks to my amazing husband, and my beautiful children, who manage to contain the pre-Christmas and birthday excitement which is threatening to burst out of them, I manage to get some time to sleep. Once we have filled up on McDonald's hash browns and hot chocolate, we head straight home and Sam insists I go up to bed.

"Everything else can wait. Get some sleep now, just a couple of hours, while you can." I know what he is saying; who knows what else might happen today. I might need my strength.

I worry that I might not be able to switch off but, once I've sunk into my soft, warm bed, and Sam has closed the curtains, I am out for the count in minutes.

I am woken by Sam gently kissing my forehead and placing a cup of coffee on the bedside table. "I'm so sorry to wake you. You looked so peaceful but—"

"Is there news?" I ask, memories hitting me head-on. "Is Dad OK?"

"No news," he soothes. "Mum rang to say Phil is much the same and Sue is OK and they're working their way through the puzzle book."

"Together? Really?"

"Yes!" he laughs. They are quite different, our mums, but they do both care about each other and they have common ground, of course, in their love for us. And I am indebted to Karen right now.

"Your mum is an angel," I say.

"I wouldn't go that far."

"Where are the kids?"

"Natalie's got the little ones and Sophie's out with Amber. Ron says Poppy is fast asleep by his fire. I think he's enjoying having her."

"So it's just you and me?" I ask.

"It certainly is."

In times past I would be pulling him into bed and pulling his clothes off. Today, I am pulling him into bed and resting my head against him, finally letting out all the pent-up anguish and emotion.

"It's OK," Sam says, one hand on my back and the other in my hair. "It's going to be OK."

"You don't know that," I sob.

"No," he admits. "I don't."

And he just lets me cry then, staying quiet while I sob, knowing there is nothing he can say to make things better. And yet he has made things better – all of them have – by everything they have done, for me and my parents. Showing me without a doubt just how much they care.

After a while I feel, if not better, slightly relieved from having let my emotions out and from having Sam's strength to prop me up. But now it's time to draw on my own strength. I might feel like staying right here under the covers, but time will stand still for no-one, and tomorrow is a double celebration in this house. Despite whatever is going on with Dad – maybe even more because of what is going on with Dad – I need to get moving. I need to make things happen.

Thankfully, Sam and I learned early in this parenting lark that it pays to wrap presents early. One Christmas Eve of last-minute disorganisation was enough to make me think again the next year. But now we have to remember where the presents are all hidden. I can't help giggling as Sam, on a stepladder, swears, rummaging around behind the suitcases on top of the wardrobe.

"There are some in the cases too," I say.

"My god, how many are there?"

"And Holly's birthday presents," I hiss, even though there is nobody else in the house to hear me. "They're in the holdall." I am excited this year to be giving Holly roller skates. I used to love mine, and the boots I graduated to when I was a bit older. Never the sportiest of children, somehow roller-skating and ice-skating seemed to suit me. There is no ice rink near here but this street is perfect for roller-skating. Nice, smooth wide pavements, and minimal traffic. I would love to be able to join her but I think I will be needed for hand-holding. We have also bought her some elbow and knee pads… "And a helmet?" I said to Sam when he came home brandishing one. "For roller-skating?" I was in danger of coming out with: "We never needed them in my day." These are suitably sensible measures though, especially when Holly is learning.

Mum has made a nose bag for the rocking horse which Dad did up for Holly last summer. Holly loves that horse.

And this year, Ben has his first gaming console. Am I happy about it? Not necessarily. But he has wanted it for – well probably just months but it feels like forever, the number of times he's mentioned it. So after talking to my parents, and Karen and Ron, Sam and I have decided he can have one, which we have all chipped in to buy. I have fretted that it's too much; that we're going to lose him to a screen. "We'll have to be strict about it," says Sam. "And it will be in the lounge so he can't have it on all the time."

It feels like yesterday that we were getting Hot Wheels and cuddly toys for Ben. How has this progression happened so fast?

Holly, for her main Christmas present, is having some animal toys that she and all her friends love at the moment. For her birthday, a woodland house for them to live in. They seem so small (I mean they are, literally tiny) in comparison to a games console, but they're bloody expensive. I'm glad she's still into toys right now though.

As ever there are far too many presents and, while we are finding them and getting organised, we can't put them out under the tree now. That has to wait till late tonight. While we wrap the last few little things for the stockings we make a few phones calls, to tell some of Mum and Dad's friends what is happening, and one to Christian to say we'd love to take up his kind offer of a Christmas and birthday dinner. He suggests we come later in the day if we can, when most of the diners will be gone and the restaurant will be quieter.

"What about your staff?" I ask. "Don't they have homes to go to and families to celebrate with?"

"Don't worry Alice, I'm not Scrooge. We'll get something worked out for you lot earlier in the day and I shall stay on to serve you personally. I was looking at Christmas on my own this year anyway, since breaking up with Sarah."

Chris has had a string of lovely, glamorous girlfriends over the years and we particularly liked Sarah but it seems he's not one for anything long-term.

"Well, will you join us and eat with us too? We can all get stuck in and lend a hand," I say.

"Alice, you're very lovely but this is meant to be easing the burden on you, not giving you more work to do. Sam, however, can be my right-hand man. You can have the seat of honour next to the birthday girl. And I'd love to join you, thank you."

I'm at that weak point where kindness like this can floor me. I dissolve into tears and I just hope that I am able to be there for the meal. Tomorrow afternoon seems a long way off yet.

Sam smiles and rubs my shoulder. "Thank you Chris. We owe you one."

In fact, I'd say we owe him more than one. Over the years, we have built up quite a large debt to Christian, the number of times he's slotted us in and let us stay way too long at his restaurant.

"My pleasure, mate."

We call Ron next. "How's it going, Ron?"

"Oh just great, thank you. I must admit I nodded off just now. When I woke up, I discovered a medium-sized dog had joined me on my chair. In fact, that is probably why I woke up. You've got a good one here, you know."

"I know." I smile. "But I was thinking Karen could maybe do with a break soon–" I wonder if Mum could do with a break from Karen too but that feels very unkind – "and I'd like to get back to the hospital for a bit."

"So we were thinking," Sam says, "would you be able to drop Poppy off and then give Alice a lift to the hospital, and pick Mum up then?"

"Of course," says Ron. "Whatever you need."

So that's one part of our plan settled.

And Sam will then collect me this evening, all being well – or assuming nothing has changed with Dad is probably more correct. I do want to be home for hanging up stockings and putting out the mince pie and carrot for Father Christmas and Rudolph. I have to try.

Again, I think of Dad, walking all that way home in the snow. He must have felt so awful that year – not just ill but still raw with grief over Grandad – but he still got himself out of bed on Christmas Eve to hang my stocking with me and put out Santa's snacks and drink. And he got up for Christmas dinner the next day. Sat with us, pulled crackers, made sure his mum was OK.

What better role model could I want?

In amongst all this, I have been trying to get hold of Julie. I have heard nothing from her since her message saying she was going in and, living on my nerves as I am right now, I am scared for her. What about those words: See you on the other side. Are they ominous? Pre-emptive? Am I over-tired, and over-thinking?

Almost certainly. But I know births are not all the same, not all straightforward, and I just hope everything is going as it should. I have messaged her back of course but the message is unread, and Luke too is not responding, but I don't suppose they're sitting there scrolling through their phones.

I have messaged Julie's Mum Cherry a few times too and she says that she had heard from Luke once or twice, early on, that things were progressing slowly but all was looking good, so she's now waiting on tenterhooks too.

I keep an eye on my phone for news of Dad or of Julie and I will try her and Luke again when I get to the hospital, before I have to switch my phone off. Surely that baby's going to arrive soon. It can't keep us waiting much longer. It is very strange to think of what Julie might be going through right now, so far away. I try to send her some strength but I don't think I have an awful lot left to go around.

At the sound of Ron's car drawing up outside, I open the front door and Poppy comes dashing into the house, up the stairs and back down, round the living room, back up the stairs and down again, her energy fully restored, it would appear. I laugh as I sit on the bottom step and she licks my face, tail wagging double-speed.

"Thank you Ron," I say to Sam's stepdad. My stepdad-in-law. "It looks like she's had an amazing time."

"Any time you want a dog sitter," he says, "I'll be happy to have her."

I kiss Sam and now I am slightly reluctant to leave the sanctuary of this house. These few hours I've been home have felt like a little pocket of time away from the real world. And while I want to see Mum and Dad, I am also scared of what I might discover.

"You'll be fine," says Sam. "And you call me any time, OK? And I'll be there at eight to pick you up, unless you tell me otherwise."

Sophie has said she'll be back home before Sam comes out to get me and she will watch *The Snowman* with Ben and Holly. That makes me feel sad because, childishly, I want to watch *The Snowman* with Ben and Holly. But needs must.

"And we'll be back in time for all the usual Christmas Eve stuff," says Sam.

"It doesn't feel like I'm going to be at the hospital for long," I say.

"No, I know. But it sounds like things are much the same. And you are under your mum's orders," he reminds me.

"I know." When I spoke to Mum she said not to come at all but she and I both knew that was not an option. I could hear the tiredness in her voice and she said it had been lovely having Karen there, but she was quite happy to have some time to herself later.

"I think you need a proper break from it all, Mum," I had said. "Away from the hospital."

"I can't leave him. Not tonight, of all nights."

"But Mum, you are going to be exhausted. You need to rest."

I will work on her while I'm there. I also don't like the thought of Dad being left alone in that great big building, but he is under excellent care, and if Mum's not careful she is going to be ill again herself.

Putting myself in her shoes though, I imagine going back home to an empty house, knowing my husband is so very ill. Could I do it, if it was Sam? I would have to, for Ben and Holly of course, but Mum doesn't have that concern. I don't really know what to do for the best. Like all of this, we will have to work it out as we go.

17.

Last night I may have thought I had got used to the sight of Dad fastened to all that medical equipment but it hits me afresh today. I gulp, and see Mum looking at me, her eyes glistening.

Hugging Karen, and thanking her, I tell her Ron is outside, and that we'll see her tomorrow.

Mum stands and embraces her. "You have been an angel, Karen," she says and I see a look pass between them. For all their differences, these two women are a similar age, and I feel that bond now between them, and it makes me feel very young, which is not something I can often say these days.

When Karen has gone, I sit with Mum and hold her hand, and she says I should hold Dad's. I do but it feels weird, and I realise I'm scared. Scared to see him like this, but *It's just Dad*, I have to remind myself. *Just my dad.*

Mum fills me in on everything that she has learned today and says that the team are happy that Dad is steady and stable.

"In fact, they are 'cautiously optimistic' – those are the words Dr Cooper used. He's so lovely, Alice."

"Mum, it's very inappropriate to have a crush on Dad's doctor!"

She smiles at this but continues, explaining that Dad will need to be on the IV drip for some time yet but they hope to be able to take him off the ventilator in the next few days, if he continues to recover well. It feels like she is an expert already and I wish I'd been here to speak to the doctors with her, but she says Karen was great and asked questions she hadn't even thought of. "And the drip is part antibiotic but also fluids, and over time the dosage will be reduced, and when your dad's able to take antibiotics orally he will."

"So they do really think he's going to get better?" I ask, less-than-cautious optimism flooding through me at the words 'when your dad's able to'.

"They don't know, Alice, being entirely honest with you. And until they can take him off the ventilator he will have to be kept sedated."

"Oh." Immediately deflated, I half-sob.

"I know." Mum's voice is flat. "It's horrible. I just want to hear his voice again. I want to hear him tell me how he is, not be second-guessing. I – I talk to him but I don't know if he can hear me."

"Mum, you need a break. You have to go home some time. You must be exhausted. I know you want to stay with Dad but you don't know how long he will be in for."

"I know. But how can I leave him?" It's Mum's turn to sob.

I realise that this must happen; some patients are so long-term, their families must have to find a way to return to some semblance of normal life and fit hospital visits in amongst everything else they have to do. "You can come home with me, Mum. Come and stay with us, if you want to."

Her eyes meet mine. "You've got a full house already, Alice. You don't need me getting in the way."

"You wouldn't be in the way."

"I would! I don't mean that in a self-pitying way but the last thing you need is somebody else to think about. Maybe I will come home tonight, but to the bungalow. I'll be alright on my own, I promise. Then I could come and see you all in the morning, see what Santa's brought, wish Holly a happy birthday, before I come back to Dad?" Mum does not look completely comfortable with this, but she needs some sleep, or at least a proper rest, in a bed. I suppose sleeping may not come easily. But it might do her good to see the kids in the morning. I know it will do them good to see her.

"That's a great idea," I say.

"I'll think about it a bit more. You haven't heard anything more from Julie, I suppose?"

"No, nothing since that message, hours and hours ago."

"Oh, well it can't be long now," Mum says brightly, and her face lights up a little, then sags again. "I hope she's not having too hard a time."

"Me too." My gaze falls to my hand, still holding Dad's. I know my shoulders are slumped.

"Hope, Alice." I look back at Mum, and it's almost like I can feel a conscious shift in her energy, seeing her rolling her shoulders back and fixing me with a look I recognise from when I was a child. She's pulling herself together, again, for me. "That's what Christmas is about, isn't it? Hope. The light in the darkness. We have to hope, that Julie delivers her baby safely, and that you hear some wonderful news from her soon. And we have to hope that your dad is strong enough to pull through this. We can't do anything about it but be here with him, and with each other, and hope."

There is silence for a while, both of us trying to keep our emotions in check. Then, awkwardly but with no clue of what else to do, I rub Dad's hand with my thumb and then gently let go of it. I pick up the puzzle book and look at Mum. "Shall we?"

"I don't think I can, love. I'm all puzzled out. Listen, I'm feeling a bit of cabin fever, do you mind sitting with Dad while I go and get some fresh air?"

"Of course not. Do you want me to come with you?"

"No, no, you stay with Phil. Please."

"OK, Mum." I don't want her going anywhere on her own but I have to respect her wishes.

And when she's gone I talk to Dad, taking his hand once more, feeling self-conscious at first but my voice growing stronger. "I hope you can hear me, Dad. Do you know what's going on? I'm here right now and Mum's just gone for a wander. She's been with you all last night, and all day today. And it's – it's Christmas Eve now. I need to go home in a while, get things set up for Ben and Holly the way you used to do for me. I wish you could be there too. Maybe we'll have another Christmas, when you're better. When you're home."

I stop speaking, settle into the quiet of the hospital room, dimly aware of the sounds of the ward outside. I'm not a religious person but I do believe in something, and I find myself closing my eyes and asking this something – whatever, whoever, it might be – not to take Dad yet. *Not yet*, I think. *We're not ready.*

Hope, I remind myself, knowing that Mum is right. It

is all we can do. While Dad is still here with us, looked after by this amazing team, his very own angels, then there is hope.

If we were on TV, this is where Dad would stir. I'd feel his hand move, or he'd open his eyes slightly, or somehow try to murmur something. But here, in the stark, clean hospital room, all I can hear is the steady, reassuring sounds of the machines and my own breath. I try and slow it down. Calm myself. Think back through Mum's words once more. The medical team are cautiously optimistic, so we must be too.

Again, I think back to Dad struggling through the snow to get home that Christmas, and imagine him now, the strength of the man inside that machine-supported body. If he can, I know he will be fighting to get through this illness and he will come home again. If he can, he will. He'll find his way back.

At this time of year, amongst the darkest of days, in so many ways, we all need to harness our hopes and hold on to them. I keep my eyes closed. Picture a Christmas candle flickering. *Light in the darkness.*

"Alice?" Mum's voice comes from the doorway. I open my eyes to see her concerned face looking at me. She has mince pies in her hands. "I brought these. They were giving them out downstairs. There are carol singers outside too."

"Really?"

"Yes, it's quite lovely. And quite emotional."

"I can imagine."

"You need to go home soon, love," she tells me, no messing.

"I don't want to leave you. Either of you."

"It's an order, I'm afraid." She smiles. I know she is right. I need to be at home. But I need to be here. I am torn.

"If you're not going home tonight, we will come and get you in the morning," I tell her.

"No it's fine, I've decided, I will go home but not till later. Karen and Ron are coming to get me, it's all arranged. I need some sleep," she says, as if I haven't been trying to tell her this exact thing. "I just spoke to Karen and she agrees."

"You two are becoming big buddies," I observe.

"She's just looking out for me, Alice. And she's a good person."

"I know."

"I will come and see you in the morning and then I'll drive myself here to see Dad."

What a way to spend Christmas Day, I think, but maybe I can convince her to join us for dinner later on. And later still, I can come and see Dad myself. Once the children are in bed or zoned out in front of the evening TV – presents open, tummies full, and hopefully a long, restful sleep ahead of them.

Even if I just have an hour with Dad tomorrow… I will find a way to make it happen. All of this is assuming nothing has changed, of course. We will just have to take things as they come.

Mum and I eat our mince pies and I make sure she has everything she needs then I take my leave, kissing her cheek and then Dad's forehead, and switching my phone on as I head out of the ward. It's hard taking the first few steps away but as I get closer to the exit, and the freshness of the Cornish night air that I know awaits me, my pace quickens.

I hear them before I see them. The carol singers are still here, and they're singing the Saint Day Carol. I can't believe I am hearing it again and I know already that whenever I hear it from now on I'll be transported back to this Christmastime.

"The first tree in the greenwood is the holly… the holly…" I can almost hear Dad singing it. And then I can hear something else: my phone ringing in my pocket.

It's Julie! And it's a video call.

"Hello?" I say, seeing my friend's face come to life on the little screen.

"Alice!" she exclaims. "Where have you been?" She doesn't wait for an answer. "There's someone I'd like you to meet."

She changes the angle of the phone to reveal the tiniest, wrinkliest little baby, with a full head of dark hair resting against her chest.

"Oh my god!" I say, laughing in spite of – or perhaps because of – everything that is going on here. "Is it—?"

"It's a baby, yes!" I hear Luke's laughing voice.

"It's a girl, Alice! We've got another little girl." Julie's smile is pure happiness.

"She hasn't got a name yet." I hear Zinnia, also off camera, and Julie turns her phone round so I can see a grinning Luke and a very composed-looking Zinnia, headphones around her neck.

"Congratulations, all of you," I say. "I am so happy for you."

"Why are you crying then?" asks Zinnia bluntly.

"These are happy tears."

"Can I hear carol singers?" Julie asks, spinning her phone back to herself, and allowing me a glimpse of the baby again.

"Yeah, I'm just–" I wonder if she can tell I'm at the hospital but I am facing towards it so behind me is just the car park – "just doing some last-minute shopping." I don't want to let on what's going on with Dad. Not now, while they are basking in the newborn glow.

"Bloody hell, that is last-minute!" she exclaims.

"Don't swear in front of the baby." I hear Luke's voice and see Julie smile across at him.

"So how was it?"

"It was – I'll tell you later," she says, and I realise she probably doesn't want to discuss it in front of Zinnia. "The important thing is, we're safe and sound, and we're all in love."

"I'm not." Zinnia's voice comes clearly.

"Ha!" I smile. "You're so lucky, Zinnie, having a sister. I always wanted one and had to make do with your mum instead. She was – she is – the closest thing I have." My words have the desired effect and I see Julie's eyes are shining.

"Our little Christmas miracle!" Luke says. "I'll leave you two to it, Zinnie's going to burst if I don't get her that hot chocolate I promised."

Julie swivels her phone round so I can see her lovely husband and daughter again.

"Bye, Luke," I say. "Bye, Zinnie. And so much love and congratulations to you all. I'm so happy for you."

The camera turns back to Julie, propped up by pillows, one arm holding that beautiful little baby close to her chest. "Alice, you're crying more than Luke did!"

"Really?" I take a moment and decide for sure I definitely won't be letting on what's happening back here. She'll never get this moment again, and there is nothing she can do anyway. "Oh Julie, I just can't tell you how delighted I am for you all."

"I'm worried about Zinnia," she says quietly. "She didn't seem very excited. What if she really does think she's any less important to us because she was adopted?"

"Julie," I say, "there is no way you and Luke will let her feel like that. I do know what you mean and it probably is a bit weird for her right now. Give her time. But even if she doesn't take to being a big sister straight away, that may be more to do with having to share you and Luke. She's had you both to herself for a long time."

I see Julie looking down, and the dreamy smile on her face, and I think of how I felt when I held my own babies that way. And how Mum and Dad will have felt at becoming parents, and their parents before them. The chain is endless and yes, babies become children, children teenagers, teenagers adults... people change and the relationship between parent and child transforms, but this is where it all begins.

Julie looks back at the screen and it's almost like we're in the same place. "I think I want to call her Hope."

I draw a breath. "That is a perfect name." She has no idea how much. "I love you Julie, I'm so proud of you. And I can't wait to have a cuddle with your little girl."

"Love you too, Alice. I'll call you tomorrow."

"When you're ready. Just take your time. And you'll be home for Christmas!"

"Fingers crossed! Love you, Griffiths. Wish you were here."

A beaming Julie disappears, taking her tiny little girl with her, and I let the tears come again, joy mingling with fear and fatigue.

Then I think of her, my beautiful friend, and her absolute, so deserved, bliss. How wonderful it is to see her so happy, after all her worries that something was wrong with her this year when all along it was the best thing possible. Life is full of surprises.

The night sky is clear and the air is still. I gaze up as I wait for Sam to arrive and whisk me back to our warm, cosy home, and I spot the North Star, shining brighter than all the others. Briefly, I close my eyes and think of Julie and Luke and Zinnia, and their new little girl, her life just beginning. Then I think of my mum and my dad. Two lots of people I love with all my heart; two hospital rooms so very far apart.

I squeeze my eyes shut then I look at the star again and I wonder if it's just too much to wish for one more Christmas miracle.

The Saint Day Carol

Also known as the Sans Day Carol and said to have been heard sung by a resident of St Day (a village not far from Redruth in Cornwall) and recorded and set to music in the early twentieth century, this beautiful carol seemed fitting for this book for a number of reasons.

Firstly, of course, it is Cornish. And I know of St Day as a place because of Gill Corbett, who this book is dedicated to. Gill and I know each other thanks to this series and her sending me a message back in 2020. Gill was living in St Day at the time. Somehow we clicked and, having never even met me, the following year Gill incredibly generously invited me and my family for a holiday. We have met a number of times since.

In the winter of 2022, when Willow – the younger of my two dogs - was a very little puppy, I was up in the night with her and the St Day Carol came on the radio. It was the first time I'd heard it, or at least really noticed it, and it brought Gill to mind, and has been a favourite ever since.

It also works particularly for this book because of the holly theme and it helps to illustrate the closeness between Alice's daughter Holly and Alice's dad.

And finally, there is the theme of motherhood and the sacrifices parents (not just mums) make for their children – as Alice's did for her, and as she and Sam now do for Sophie, Ben and Holly.

Now the holly bears a berry as white as the milk,
And Mary bore Jesus, who was wrapped up in silk:

And Mary bore Jesus Christ our Saviour for to be,
And the first tree in the greenwood, it was the holly.
Holly! Holly!
And the first tree in the greenwood, it was the holly!

Now the holly bears a berry as green as the grass,
And Mary bore Jesus, who died on the cross:

And Mary bore Jesus Christ our Saviour for to be,
And the first tree in the greenwood, it was the holly.
Holly! Holly!
And the first tree in the greenwood, it was the holly!

Now the holly bears a berry as black as the coal,
And Mary bore Jesus, who died for us all:

And Mary bore Jesus Christ our Saviour for to be,
And the first tree in the greenwood, it was the holly.
Holly! Holly!
And the first tree in the greenwood, it was the holly!

Now the holly bears a berry, as blood is it red,
Then trust we our Saviour, who rose from the dead:

And Mary bore Jesus Christ our Saviour for to be,
And the first tree in the greenwood, it was the holly.
Holly! Holly!
And the first tree in the greenwood, it was the holly!

Acknowledgements

I will start with an apology to anyone who was looking for a very specifically happy ending to this book! It was a difficult decision for me to leave the story at the point where it is, and particularly bearing in mind that this is a Christmas book. But I do have my reasons!

I can't tell you how much I love writing this series and slipping back into Alice's shoes. I do want you all to feel uplifted by the books but sometimes it's not in the most obvious of ways. As Alice mentions briefly, it's usually down to the likes of the soap operas to bring the drama at Christmas, and it does annoy me sometimes, but at the same time I did not want to wrap this book up with an unrealistic ending.

I hope I've found a balance, with Julie and Luke's wonderful news, and the way that Alice's friends and family rally around. I see this book as a tale of love, hope and community in adversity, and I hope that it can be heartwarming for those reasons even if we would all have loved Phil to make a miraculous recovery just in time for the Big Day.

And on to my round of THANK YOUs – which, given the timescale of developing this book, are even more deserved than ever! To the following Christmas stars:

Catherine Clarke, you have pulled it out of the bag yet again, and I love this beautiful cover, and your ingenious solution to the longer-than-usual title! Thank you for everything.

My amazing, incredible, and generous team of beta-readers: Julie Meadows, Tracey Shaw, Rebecca Leech, Marilynn Wrigley, Jean Crowe, Alison Lassey, Kate Jenkins, Ginnie Ebbrell, Amanda Tudro, Roz Osborn, Mandy Chowney-Andrews, Helen Smith, Hilary Kerr, Denise Armstrong, Sandra Francis and Julie Moxham.

I am forever grateful for your help, honesty, support and positivity – and thought-provoking feedback! I know this book has divided opinion with some of you, and it's shorter than normal, but I hope in 2026 its place in the scheme of things will make more sense as I hope you will be reviewing the continuation of this series before too long ☺

To Gill – thank you. And you are never far from my thoughts. May 2026 find a way to bring some brightness back for you.

And to all of my readers, old and new. THANK YOU. So much. What a total honour it is to know that people are reading my books and hopefully enjoying them too! I love hearing from all of you, whether it's a comment on Facebook, a message on Instagram, an email… if you feel the urge to do so, you are very welcome to drop me a line: katharine@heddonpublishing.com

Wishing all of you a very happy Christmas and a peaceful, happy and healthy 2026.

Kath xx

Coming Back to Cornwall

The bestselling series that refuses to end!

The whole Coming Back to Cornwall series is being made into audiobooks so you that you can listen to the adventures of Alice, Julie and Sam while you drive, cook, clean, go to sleep... whatever, wherever! Books One to Five are available now.

Connections
Books One to Four

Each story focuses on a different character all inextricably linked within the small Cornish town they call home.

What Comes Next

This short, festive story is an exploration of another side of this time of year normally packed with family, friends and festivities. It is nevertheless uplifting and engaging, and full of Christmas spirit.

As her family begin to find their way through their grief and navigate new situations and changing relationships, Ruth herself has much to learn as she comes to terms with her new situation and the fact that she can now only watch as life moves on without her.

The focus moves to Annie in this second full-length novel of the series – to work and pregnancy and motherhood, and everything in between. Self-discovery is key as life changes in so many unimaginable ways.

Individual novels

Writing the Town Read: Katharine's first novel. "I seriously couldn't put it down and would recommend it to anyone who doesn't like chick lit, but wants a great story."

Looking Past - a story of motherhood and growing up without a mother.

"Despite the tough topic the book is full of love, friendships and humour. Katharine Smith cleverly balances emotional storylines with strong characters and witty dialogue, making this a surprisingly happy book to read."

Amongst Friends - a back-to-front tale of friendship and family, set in Bristol.

"An interesting, well written book, set in Bristol which is lovingly described, and with excellent characterisation. Very enjoyable."

www.ingramcontent.com/pod-product-compliance
Lightning Source LLC
Chambersburg PA
CBHW032004180726
48283CB00008B/2570